Thomas Creeper and the Gloomsbury Secret

J.R. Potter

with illustrations by the author

Fitzroy Books

Published by Fitzroy Books
An imprint of
Regal House Publishing, LLC
Raleigh, NC 27612

https://fitzroybooks.com

Printed in the United States of America

ISBN -13 (paperback): 9781646030590
ISBN -13 (epub): 9781646030842
Library of Congress Control Number: 2020941105

Interior and cover design by Lafayette & Greene
lafayetteandgreene.com

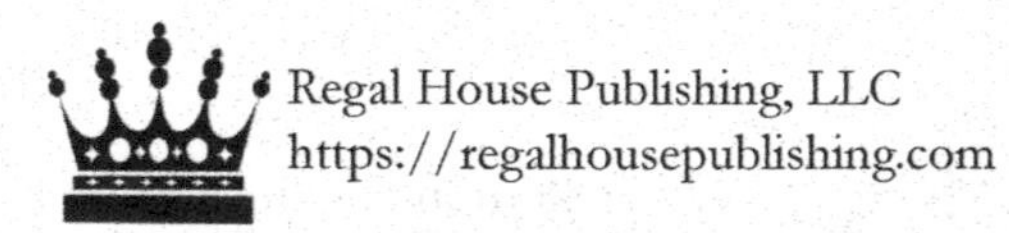

Regal House Publishing, LLC
https://regalhousepublishing.com

Printed in the United States of America

For my niece and nephew, Mara and Liem,
and my godchildren, Max and Violet.
May your own adventures be greater than any story
and filled with love and joy that overthrows all monsters.

And to the memory of the late-great John Bellairs (1938-1991)
whose stories changed a ten-year-old boy's life forever.

CONTENTS

The Conch Whistle Rises 1

PART ONE: 3

A Death & Two Sightings, One Not So Welcome 5

The Creeper Family Diary 29

Ms. Katz Pulls a Black and White Photograph 49

Forensic Science, A Detective's Best Weapon 63

PART TWO 76

"Hello, boy!" 79

Combine or Die 95

Mary Looks at Caesar 107

"Not in That Much Pain" 119

As Constant and as Old As Time 131

PART THREE 140

Custodians and Preservers 143

The Lady, the Weapon 161

Wild Death 175

Worms 187

A Friend Team 197

Unfinished Business 205

Thomas Creeper and the Purple Corpse 215

"The ghost of 'lectricity howls in the bones of her face…"

— Bob Dylan, "Visions of Johanna"

"Don't go looking under rocks."

— Old Gloomsbury saying

Prologue

The Conch Whistle Rises

Out in the rolling deep something stirred.

Though no starlight or moonlight pierced the dense veil of clouds ringing Gloomsbury Bay, a faint glow—emerald green and pink—coming from signal lights attached to the large channel markers, broke through the swirling fog. Just beyond the light of one bobbing channel marker a copper periscope lifted from the water, kelp and seaweed clinging to its far-seeing eye.

The metal eye turned in the direction of the land: to the swaying cattail marshes, and beyond them, to the twinkling lights of Gloomsbury, Massachusetts, the cursed town. *Gloomsbury.* The town where the sun never shone but once or twice a year; where a stranglehold of clouds from a weather system dubbed "Mad Marge" by old sailors choked out warmth and sunlight, leaving the residents of the small seaside town pale and depleted of Vitamin D. Gloomsbury, of mold and tide pools where life rushed in...but didn't always get out.

The periscope lowered. Up from the wine-dark sea the submersible now rose, its giant copper frame like a metallic whale breaching. From the viewing deck in the center of the submersible's body a hatch flung open. Two figures crawled out—one tall and broad-shouldered, the other as short as he was wide. The smaller, squatter figure struck a waterproof match against the hatch door and for a brief instant his face flared out of the darkness, yellow-green and speckled with spots like a frog. The light of the match moved upward from the strange amphibious face to light a pipe in the hands of the taller figure next to him.

"Thank you, Mouth," said the man, leaning down and taking a few swift draws on the pipe until the bowl was sufficiently smoking. The pipe bowl glowed a bright orange, illuminating the contours of the man's face: square jaw, blond beard, and a deep red scar—in the shape of three claw marks—that ran the length of his cheek. For a few moments the two figures stood in silence while the submersible—their movable home and museum of all the wonders they had found exploring the world—rocked gently against the waves beneath them. Overhead a seagull broke the silence with its shrill cry. It flew out over the submersible, away from the shoreline. Even birds had an opinion about Gloomsbury it seemed. The man on the deck took a few more puffs from his pipe and reaching down, patted the shoulder of the creature named Mouth who had just spied a large June bug whizzing by.

Without a moment's hesitation, the creature lashed out his long, whip-like tongue, consuming the buzzing insect and living up to the reputation of his name.

"Do you think the boy has any clue how terrible it's going to get?" the man whispered, gesturing toward the shoreline with his pipe. "What those…*monsters* are going to do to him? There are far too many of them, Mouth. Dug into the whole rotting edifice like termites! And as for rumors of the Weapon.…" The man grimaced and spat over the side of the ship. "History has not smiled favorably on those in his family who have tried to keep it safe."

But Mouth didn't speak. The things Mouth ate told him about places—it was his special gift. He could eat a shoe and tell you every street the shoe had gone down. The bug moving from his throat to his large-chambered stomach told him what the seagull fleeing the shoreline would have told him if only his tongue could stretch that high. But the message was clear:

Terrible things were afoot.

BOOK ONE:
The Phantom Car & The Girl on the Stairs
CREEPER
SONS
FUNERAL
HOME
892117

GO AHEAD
TRY IT.
JR

I

A Death & Two Sightings, One Not So Welcome

Thomas Creeper was late.

As the son of Gloomsbury's only mortician, time was always "of the essence," as the saying went.

A fresh corpse left too long would become as heavy as a giant, unbendable tree limb. The only difference is that the tree limb used to be your fifth-grade teacher, Mrs. Hanson, or your neighbor whose face you saw only when they bent back the blinds to make sure you weren't tromping down their flower beds.

Thirteen-year-old Thomas Creeper knew Gloomsbury Township inside and out. He knew the roads like Shellburne, with its winding flood walls topped with oyster shells, where they used to turn shells into cement over a century ago; the marshes like Sarah's Lament, where the widow Sarah Belkerstein disappeared one night in her bathrobe, believing she'd heard the sound of her husband's Navy ship returning from the war. Thomas knew, too, about the dangerous sinkholes. (We will get to them soon enough. For now, just make a mental note: *sinkholes = very bad.* You could even imagine a giant skull next to the word if you'd like.)

But what was even worse was that because of Thomas's job as mortician's apprentice he knew the *people* of Gloomsbury Township inside and out. He knew their secret moles and birthmarks, their rare diseases, even what they last ate for dinner before they passed away. Believe me, there are not enough iPad games of crushing candy or catapulting birds to rid your brain of all that gooey and revolting stuff.

And if dealing with cadavers and bodily functions wasn't bad enough, of all days of the year when a legitimate "sun sighting" was predicted by all the local weather channels, Thomas Creeper was running late.

He hit the corner where the two main arteries of Gloomsbury crossed—Thayer Street and Weiland Avenue. Here the cement turned to wet and moldy cobblestones that caused cars to jostle and lurch into hydraulic spaz machines as they bumped their way toward the once-grand thoroughfare of Weiland Avenue and its splinter-fest of a boardwalk that led down to Town Beach. The rain, which fell nearly 363 days of the year, had let up a little…*a little*. But it was still a misting mess of a Wednesday in the middle of June. Only a few days earlier Thomas had graduated from Gloomsbury Middle School, home of the Fighting Squids. In addition to co-captaining the chess team, Thomas had ended his career as a Fighting Squid as a once-in-a-blue-moon standout for the school's track team.

He had hit his growth spurt earlier that year, sprouting a whole four inches in three months. Now he looked like a gangly, black-haired weed with a pale, pinched face like an albino squash. If his gangly legs were any gift at all, they helped him run away from the funeral home that was also his house. Try as he might, however, he could never outrun the horrible fact that he slept in a house with dead people.

Rounding the deserted bus terminal at Thayer and Weiland, he nearly stepped head-first into the path of a rust-colored sedan that blared its horn as it rocketed past, splashing gutter water all over Thomas's shirt and new glasses.

"You're gonna miss it!" a weaselly kid with his two front teeth missing shouted at him from the back window of the speeding car. Muttering and cursing to himself, Thomas wiped the lenses of his glasses with the side of his shirttail, blood roaring in his ears. He checked the time on his trusty Ken Darby Spy Watch complete with retractable wire (peppermint floss), an infrared message decoder (broken since

Christmas), and a hidden tray of cyanide pills (licorice for health reasons; c'mon, people!).

6:14 p.m... Two minutes!

The weasel-faced kid was right. He was going to miss it.

He flew down Weiland Avenue like a boy on fire. Jumping in between cars he leapt up onto the opposite sidewalk but landed flatfooted on the wet bricks, twisting his left ankle. *Was the whole world conspiring against him today?* He gnashed his teeth from the pain, blew a ragged breath through his nostrils, and fought his way forward, dragging his sprained foot like a crutch toward the smell of salt air and the screeching of the gulls up ahead.

It seemed as if the whole town had assembled to watch the sun sighting. It wasn't a mystery that the town of Gloomsbury was cursed. It was right there in the name.

Between the horrible weather system "Mad Marge" that encircled the town, to the vast network of underground sinkholes that could pull whole cars or baby carriages unexpectedly down to their doom, Gloomsbury was the least valued real estate in all of Massachusetts.

Even the neighboring town called Marvale had a better reputation. It had seceded from Gloomsbury in the 1920s like a broken hip, boasting to this day, "No Stinkin' Sinkholes." It wasn't the greatest town motto. But it was still better than Gloomsbury's:

"Live Here, Work Here, Die Here."

Thomas scanned the boardwalk all the way to the empty lifeguard tower on Town Beach. He could never remember anyone ever *actually* trying to swim in Gloomsbury Bay. There were unexpected riptides and discarded lobster pots that could ensnare your ankle, not to mention the occasional great white shark up from Provincetown that always spiced things up. At the door of the boarded-up lifeguard station a spray-painted sign hung for all to see.

"**GO AHEAD. TRY IT,**" the sign read.

Thomas could see all the regular faces assembled for the sun sighting: there was Eugenia Sneed, of the wealthy Sneeds who lived up on the bluffs high above Gloomsbury on a great estate called Ivymount that no outsiders, not even telephone repairmen, had set foot on in years; there was Mr. Marsden, the town postman, his chin pushed all the way back, gazing up at the clouds, the fat ripples rippling down the back of his neck; there was Ms. Katz, the town librarian, with her two greyhounds that suffered from a rare skin disease that made them hairless and eternally itchy; and there was the parish staff of the local Catholic Church, St. Mary's by the Sea, ready to call the event "an act of divine Providence." Next to them Thomas could see the new family he hadn't met yet at church with the young daughter with the frizzy hair like electrified snakes. But no Jeni. *Where in the world was Jeni Myers?*

"Hey, gimpy! Over here!"

Thomas craned his neck, trying to see over the murmuring crowd. But as he swiveled around too fast on his stilt-like legs, he lost his balance…and ran smack into a mountain of chest and arms! Adjusting his glasses from where they had slipped on his nose, he blinked his eyes a few times expecting to see the worst: Gary Korvin, resident wedgie-wringer, earlobe-flicker, and infamous locker-smearer (the Korvins had a pond out in front of their house frequented each season by geese). Thomas relaxed…*a little*. It was just Mr. Contenescu, who ran the day-to-day operations at Sneed Waste Removal Services. People whispered around town that the old Romanian had once been a bare-knuckle boxing champion, but that he'd been banished from the sport for biting someone's throat. No substantial proof had yet to surface to confirm or deny the rumor.

"S-s-sorry," Thomas stammered in apology while Mr. Contenescu stared down at him from behind a thick, black moustache, wide as a skunk's tail but without the white stripe. The expression on the old Romanian's face was indecipherable: indeed, a stone wall had more to say. After running his darting, black eyes over Thomas for a few more seconds—during which Thomas contemplated whether a swift uppercut would come out of nowhere, launching him backwards over the lifeguard stand into the treacherous waters of Gloomsbury Bay—Mr. Contenescu finally stepped aside. Thomas exhaled sweet relief. He blinked his eyes, and when he unblinked them there she was: standing in front of him, shaking her head at him with that same Jeni Myers smile that was always part smile, part jeer, depending on how you looked at it.

"Don't worry," said Jeni. "You didn't miss it. Look!"

Above the white-capped sea the black sky began to lighten. The army of clouds patrolling Gloomsbury Bay momentarily gave up their stranglehold. The crowd let out a resounding "*AHHHHHHHHHH!*" and for the first time in seven months, twelve days, six hours, and thirty-two minutes the sun shone down upon Gloomsbury Township—on the rusting square and compass on the Masonic Lodge, on the mossy headstones and shrieking gargoyles in Gloomsbury Cemetery, on the salt crusted cars, and most importantly, on Thomas Creeper himself.

The light shimmered like a golden veil tossed from some high astral plain where things never rot but bloom eternally. Mr. Marsden, whose sagging face tied off in a grimace at the bottom like the knot of a balloon, radiated a rare beam of joy; Ms. Katz, tears welling in her eyes, threw her arms around her hairless greyhounds until their powerful dander made her neck start to itch; even sour-faced Eugenia Sneed, who was just about to flick the cigarette butt from her long-stemmed cigarette holder into the inky surf, paused and looked agape at the miraculous vision of the sun shining down on the moldy, barnacled town she had given her life to without so much as a thank-you, only a few fading plaques in the Sneed name and a tax break or two to pay for a new wing of her mansion devoted solely to teacups.

Like an intermission in the horrible drama of his life, Thomas felt everything that was weighing him down suddenly lift—the dampness in his lungs, the funeral home where his father would be waiting for him with whatever new body had just arrived. But then the clouds sealed back overhead. The light faded. The crowd let out a mournful sigh. The news crew lowered their cameras. Eugenia flicked her cigarette into the surf and slid back through the open door of her pearly white Jaguar (which only she and she alone was allowed to park so close to the beach, having paid for the Great Sludge Removal of 1994). The Jaguar squealed away, spitting sand and clouds of choking exhaust. The world as Thomas Creeper knew it returned to its regular miserable programming.

Once the last glimmer of light had officially receded, the residents began their depressed march back up the boardwalk. As the crowd thinned out, Jeni stepped closer to Thomas, a finger propped up under her chin. She looked him over, head to toe, a curious expression on her face like someone scrutinizing a police lineup.

"That's it! I knew something was different!" Jeni exclaimed. "You got new glasses! You look...*professorial!*"

"I don't think that's even a word," said Thomas, blushing faintly. *Of course, it was a word!* he thought. Jeni Myers was even smarter than him. He quickly changed the subject. "Where's Arnold?" he asked.

"Probably blowing something up at home," sighed Jeni. "Do you know he did his Concepts of Physics pressurized rocket experiment *inside* the house?"

"Sounds like Arnold," said Thomas. *He had to ask her...*an image of himself with his pale legs standing all alone in the middle of Splashdown Waterpark flashed inside his brain. "Hey..." he began, gathering his courage. "I was wondering. Are you...it's no big deal if you aren't but...are you going with the teen group to Splashdown Mountain this weekend? I was thinking maybe we could—"

"You didn't hear?" said Jeni, cutting him off. "Oh my god. I'm such a jerk! I totally forgot to tell you! The trip's been canceled. Pop Mulvaney—"

Suddenly, out of nowhere, a tower of legs and arms knocked into Thomas.

He was the tallest boy at Gloomsbury Middle School, taller even than Thomas. His height advantage seemed to give him a free pass to push others aside like a tropical jungle explorer thrashing his way through tall vegetation...only the vegetation happened to be people. When the tall boy made it through a few bodies he looked back and flashed Thomas a wicked grin. Thomas felt his stomach muscles seize up and tighten. It was Gary Korvin.

I'm sure you know a Gary Korvin in your town or even at your own school. He might be named Larry—Larry Morvin, or Harry Foreman. But he's the worst. He's the worst because someone *made* him that way—a brother, a parent, a father who wasn't around—and now someone can't *unmake* him. Thomas would never forget the time at the Gloomsbury Pumpkin Festival when Gary pulled an iron rake out of a scarecrow's hands and told Thomas to "run from his fiery javelin." No big surprise, Thomas made it about ten feet before the rake hit him behind the knees, and he went down like a lassoed cow. Thomas prayed Jeni didn't hear what Gary said as he passed by snickering today...but Thomas had heard it, and the words made his fists ball up at his sides:

Out of the way, Creepy Thomas!

It was the name Thomas couldn't outrun, even with all his track team skills. It followed him everywhere like dog poop in the tread of his sneaker. He had learned to ignore it, but there were some days—mostly after sticking his hands inside a dead body—when the mental armor he had to wear just to be him, just to be alive in his own skin, got worn down so thin that even a wrong look could set him off. As soon as he turned eighteen, he swore he was going to change his name. No Gary Korvin or Barry Torpin would ever taunt him again. He had already picked out his new name: Chase Radley. (C'mon, admit it! You already want to be friends with Chase Radley!).

Fortunately for Thomas, Jeni didn't hear Gary, or if she did, she ignored him.

"It's horrible," she went on. "I overheard my mom talking on the phone last night. They think Pop died in his sleep. Heart attack, that's what Mrs. Grossman says. Oh, Thomas. It's horrible. They canceled the trip because of the funeral this weekend."

Thomas's breath caught in his lungs. He stared back at Jeni for a few seconds, feeling numb all over, and when the numbness fell away, a hollowness in the center of his chest. Pop was dead? The words didn't make sense, but that's what Jeni had said. Pop couldn't be dead. Pop Mulvaney was the only priest at St. Mary's he actually liked. He told silly jokes and made a point of shaking everybody's hand after Sunday services, even standing in the rain so he didn't miss anyone. Sure, he was old—*grandparent*-old. But he was always there, always around, always smiling and waving outside the giant carved oak doors of St. Mary's or pacing the flagstones trying to find the right words for his Sunday sermon. And now he was gone, just like that. Like the last glimmer of light sucked out over Gloomsbury Bay.

Thomas and Jeni turned and left the beach, following the other stragglers up the boardwalk and back onto Weiland Avenue. When they hit the corner that looked up at the eternally vacant Fisherman's Haven Hotel, Jeni placed a hand on Thomas's arm.

"Are you going to be okay?" she asked, this time without the slightest hint of Jeni Myers sarcasm behind her voice.

"I'm fine," said Thomas, brushing away the arm before Gary or anyone else could see it. "I better get home. I'm sure my dad is already writing my evening list."

Suddenly, one of the windows in the hotel above their heads *thwapped* open.

A paunchy man in half-buttoned overalls, with a massive beard the color of an unwashed golden poodle, poked his head out of the open window holding an orange tabby cat in his outstretched arms. Thomas and Jeni watched dumbstruck as the man proceeded to place the growling cat on the ledge outside the window, then slammed the window shut. As if accustomed to this ritual, the cat sat back on the ledge, happy as a clam, and proceeded to clean itself in the misting rain.

"C'mon," said Jeni. "I'll walk back with you." A smile stretched across her pale face—*pale and freckled*, but not pinched like Thomas's. A beautiful face. Thomas might tell her someday, if saying it out loud didn't make his stomach turn over on itself.

"Don't want you to twist the other ankle," she added with a giggle.

"Very funny," said Thomas.

They walked back through the wet cobblestone streets, past Gloomsbury Treats on Thirty-Third and Weiland where they might have stopped for some Mad Marge Marzipan or Shark Tooth Taffy, if Thomas's father wasn't already waiting for him. No doubt Thomas's father, Elijah Creeper the Fifth, would be standing at the large bay window of their old Victorian house, tapping his gold-rimmed glasses impatiently against the windowsill. The image made Thomas cringe because he couldn't ignore the fact:

He was the spitting image of his father.

He knew it was his destiny to grow as tall and gaunt as Elijah Creeper the Fifth, like all male Creepers who threw themselves into their horrible work, night and day, each one stoop-shouldered from perpetually leaning over corpses.

There would come a time when someone wouldn't be able to tell the difference between Thomas and his father (besides a few more wrinkles in his father's face or gray in his beard). That would be the day Thomas took over the funeral home, the day of his inheritance. But Thomas wasn't supposed to be the heir. That wasn't the plan. David, who'd loved science and never—not even once—cringed at the sight of a dead body, was supposed to have taken over as Gloomsbury's sole mortician.

But David had died a year ago in his sleep, from what Dr. Filch—the town's quack—had insisted was a heart attack. Thomas supposed there could have been some truth in the diagnosis—who knew how often heart murmurs went undetected, anyway, even in kids?—if it weren't for the manner in which Dr. Filch had inspected the body. Brandishing the withered remains of an Egyptian hand, the elderly doctor proclaimed that the artifact would point "like a magnetic beacon to the source of David's mortal illness." To make matters worse, the morning after David's death, Thomas's father insisted that Thomas help him prepare David's body for the funeral. Thomas still hadn't forgiven his father for that.

At the intersection of Thayer and Mt. Parnassus—a street that divided the section of Gloomsbury known unofficially as The Uppercrust, the wealthy neighborhood where Jeni's family lived, from the poorer section, Thayer Row, where the Creepers resided—Jeni gave Thomas a hug.

"I'll see you Friday at Pop's funeral," she told him.

Thomas bit his lip and peered down at the wet ground. The cobblestones blurred under his feet. He could feel the tears brimming at the edges of his eyes, just waiting to ruin everything. He could hear Jeni's voice…but it wasn't Pop he was thinking about anymore, not this close to the wretched funeral home. That's what Jeni didn't understand. There was something else—*someone else*—gnawing at his heart.

"I know you liked Pop. We all did. But he was old, Thomas. I know that doesn't make it easier. Maybe…maybe he didn't feel any pain. Maybe he just went to bed and—"

"It's not just Pop!" Thomas growled, blinking back hot tears. Jeni's face snapped back into focus. "I saw her again, Jen! The girl on the stairs! I'm telling you she's *real.* I don't want to go back in there. I know she'll be waiting for me…."

Thomas trailed off. The misting rain had turned to a heavy patter. Rain trickled beneath his collar, chilling him down to his bones.

"She's not there, Thomas," said Jeni. She brushed a few wet strands of strawberry blonde hair out of her face until Thomas could see her flashing green eyes shining through the gloom. "Ghosts aren't real, Thomas. Dead bodies are."

"What's that supposed to mean?" Thomas shot back. *What was she trying to get at? Why would she make things worse by saying something so stupid?*

Jeni shrugged. "All I mean is that the dead can't hurt you. If they could we'd all be in trouble. Wouldn't you be angry at someone who could do all the things you couldn't do anymore?"

"I guess so," said Thomas. "Like organizing jars of formaldehyde…polishing caskets…."

"You know what I mean," said Jeni flashing him a sour look. But the sour look didn't last long. A toothy smile broke over Jeni's freckled face. "Cheer up, professor!" she cried, patting Thomas on the shoulder. "How about this? Why don't we go to Sal's for pizza after my soccer practice tomorrow? We can steal some of Arnold's fireworks if you have time before tackling your list. And check your email when you get home! I sent you another cipher. I went all out on this one. Just saying…."

Walking away, she glanced back over her shoulder, flashing him a brilliant smile.

A perfect Jeni Myers smile.

"Cool!" Thomas shouted back, brightening a little. "See you later!"

He waved goodbye to Jeni and turned back down Thayer. As if right on cue, guaranteed to quash all happiness and joy, Thomas spied the speeding car careening around the street corner, his weird uncle Jed bobbing in the driver's seat. The car was sleek and black like a panther and as long as a speedboat. Flying down the street, oblivious to potholes and cobblestones, came the Creeper family's 1957 Ford Star Model Customline hearse, which they used for all pickups and deliveries. The car honked at Thomas as it flew past, the horn blaring like a mournful goose. A few seconds later the antique hearse slipped out of view, headed for the back entrance of the funeral home—which meant only one thing:

They had a delivery. And Thomas was pretty sure he knew who it was.

He sighed again into his damp collar and trudged down the block until he could feel the shadow of the great house up ahead, its sign swaying precariously from the signpost out front, barely secured by its rusted hinges:

Creeper & Sons Funeral Home
Est. 1878

Behind the mold-speckled sign and rotting gate the old Victorian house loomed like some great black bird, its moldy shingles overlapping one another like feathers on a crow's back. A thick grove of oak and cypress trees surrounded the house, preventing any chance of light from filtering in through the moth-eaten curtains. As Thomas made his way up the sinking flagstone path, mud oozing out from beneath the moss-covered stones with every step, he kept his eyes averted from the figure waiting for him on the porch. It wasn't his father, nor any *living* person for that matter. It was something dead that didn't seem to want to stay that way.

"You aren't real, you aren't real…" Thomas repeated over and over like a protective chant as he gripped the chipped porch railing and began to climb. "Jeni's right. I can't see you. You don't exist."

But he knew he was seeing the girl on the steps—even if Jeni didn't believe him. Ghosts did exist. They were everywhere. They were real as shadows were real, even if you couldn't touch them. And one ghost in particular lived in the funeral home, right alongside Thomas Creeper.

Sometimes Thomas would glimpse her on the porch,

other times in the hallway, standing next to the wooden pedestal that held the large, leatherbound Creeper family diary with entries dating all the way back to the 1800s. The nights when he wasn't at school or assisting his father in the Preparing Room, Thomas would go to the wooden pedestal and flip through the yellowed and cracked pages of the diary, hoping to find something to make her go away—anything, some secret, some clue to the puzzle of why she haunted the old house.

But he never found it. She would disappear for weeks—months sometimes—and then, suddenly, she would appear right next to him, staring back at him with the same stricken expression on her face, her arms folded behind her, hidden within the folds of her dress, her mouth open as if to speak…though no words ever came out.

"Leave me alone," said Thomas, climbing up the last rotting steps onto the porch.

But the girl didn't move.

Thomas walked right through her, as if she were nothing more than a damp cloud. The death chill surged through his veins, as if he had been dunked into a freezing lake for a split second, then hauled out by his shoulders, shivering. Fighting off chatters in his teeth, he pulled back the screen door and stepped into the musty foyer, teeming with all the horribly familiar smells: the maroon-colored drapes that reeked of mold; the eternal stench of formaldehyde and embalming fluid from the Preparing Room; and the lingering odor of grease that had accompanied whatever beef monstrosity of a meal his mother had recently concocted.

"What happened to your leg?" a deep voice boomed out from the shadows.

"Nothing!" Thomas hollered back.

"Nothing?"

Out of the shadows, into a patch of light cast by the flickering chandelier over the foyer, Elijah Creeper the Fifth stepped forward.

At over six and a half feet tall, Thomas's father cast what people call "a long shadow." Bony and thin as a rail, he resembled a giant grasshopper-human hybrid with glittering black eyes magnified to three times their ordinary size behind glasses with large prescription lenses and long white fingers that were perpetually cold, regardless of the season. There were words that never managed to fight their way to Thomas's father's lips—words that could save rotting relationships—such as, *I love you. I'm sorry. Forgive me. I didn't mean to say all those horrible things....*

"Well, at least that explains you being late!" snapped Elijah Creeper the Fifth, removing an antique pipe from his waistcoat pocket and proceeding to pack strong-smelling tobacco into the bowl. "Why are you always dilly-dallying around town, Thomas? Can't you see we have—"

"A delivery, I know," sighed Thomas. He winced. He knew better than to cut his father off. But he wasn't in the mood to follow Creeper Family Protocol that required the utmost attention and respect between son and father, apprentice and master, but never the other way around. Thomas could feel the lecture coming on, so he clamped it off—as if his father's tirade were a gushing artery. "I saw Uncle Jed's car!" he added quickly. "It's Pop Mulvaney, isn't it?"

Mr. Creeper's eyes narrowed to two black slants behind his smudged glasses as he regarded his son and sole apprentice with pursed lips. The tobacco bowl neatly packed, he lit a match. Bright light flared across his gaunt face. Thomas felt terror wash over him. There was no doubt in his mind: He was looking at himself in thirty years, maybe not even that long!

"Mask and gloves! Five minutes!" bellowed Elijah Creeper the Fifth. Without another word, he turned on his heel and strode down the long hallway toward the Preparing Room, a stream of pipe smoke wafting in his wake.

Letting out another deep sigh, Thomas turned to follow but was brought to an abrupt halt when his eyes caught a reflection in the foyer mirror. The ghost-girl was peering in at him through the curtains of the bay window that looked out onto the rickety porch.

"Go away," he said and turned and headed down the dark hallway.

❧

The cooling board consisted of a large gray slab of metal that pulled out from a temperature-controlled cooler. The cooler, and the board on which the body rested, helped slow the rate of decomposition of a fresh corpse so that the mortician had time to cover any wounds and restore the body to a state in which it looked almost alive, as if the person were merely sleeping.

In the old days, as Thomas's father often reminded him, before temperature-controlled refrigeration, bodies had been kept on giant blocks of ice that dripped everywhere, or at the bottom of root cellars where an unsuspecting stumbler, searching perhaps for a rutabaga or parsnip, might have the shock of their life grabbing hold of stiff fingers already in *rigor mortis*.

(Rigor mortis, in case you didn't already know, is the stiffening that immediately happens to a corpse after the heart stops pumping blood. Think of a well-done steak left out in the snow for a couple of days and you'll get the picture.)

Thomas's father constantly went on and on about "the wonder of refrigeration," what he proclaimed to be "the mortician's greatest ally in the race against The Warm!" often letting his voice fall to a dramatic hush on the last two words. *The Warm*...Thomas always cringed when he heard that. *The Warm*—it was like something out of an old black-and-white horror film where happy, well-meaning people slowly got melted down by some mad scientist's heat laser.

The Preparing Room, where corpses were treated and embalmed, was about as cheery and warm as the North Pole at midnight. Tonight, as Thomas and his father set to work on

Pop Mulvaney, Thomas was sure he'd be able to see his own breath if his sanitary mask hadn't been covering his mouth. The chill numbed his brain and turned the tips of his fingers bone white. It was as if the air knew how to get inside him, chilling him from the inside out—worse, even, than passing through the ghost-girl on the stairs. He tried to focus on his duties, to follow his father's orders, but this time was harder than usual...the corpse, after all, had once been his friend.

Blinking back tears, he gazed down at the body of Pop Mulvaney. He reminded himself that the thing on the table wasn't Pop Mulvaney anymore. He tried to smile, thinking of the old priest as he had been in life—kind Pop Mulvaney, who had picked Thomas up with one arm after he'd skinned his knee, telling him jokes while he fished through the church's medical kit for a Band-Aid; Pop Mulvaney, who brought homemade cinnamon buns and hot chocolate to the teen group's volunteer day; Pop Mulvaney, who once read a poem by an English poet during Sunday service instead of rattling off some stuffy old sermon.

No, thought Thomas, a hard knot forming in his throat. The cold, blue-lipped thing on the table wasn't Pop Mulvaney anymore. It was just his shell. Just as a cicada's shell hangs on a tree before it takes to the wind....

A clatter of metal sounded behind Thomas, startling him.

"What have you done with the aspirator, Elijah Thomas?" his father's voice boomed. "How many times must I tell you," Elijah Creeper the Fifth seethed, waving a bony finger in the air like a dagger, "that a mortician's tools should always be returned to their precise location in the event—"

"'A situation calls for accelerated measures to arrest decomposition,'" Thomas contributed wearily. It was one of the tenets of the Creeper Family Protocol, a doctrine as stony and staunch as the Ten Commandments. Thomas spied the aspirator beneath a stack of newspapers and silently handed it to his father, who fumed in silence, his menacing expression hidden behind the light of the medical lamp shining down on the corpse. Thomas hated those kinds of tense silences in the Preparing Room. Some nights it was even worse—his father would take a pause in his lecture just long enough for a corpse to emit a "death rattle," the escaping of a pocket of air through the body cavity or lungs. Nothing fun about that.

Elijah Creeper the Fifth approached the corpse, wielding the autopsy aspirator—a long instrument the size and shape of a child's bent elbow that could be mistaken for something used, perhaps, for injecting pastry cream into cakes…if only the Creepers had been bakers. The aspirator did nothing so sweet. It removed blood and fluid from a corpse, and the many holes along its sides ensured that nothing got clogged up during this ghastly process.

"What's going on with you and that Myers girl?" Mr. Creeper asked suddenly, positioning the aspirator over Pop Mulvaney's carotid artery. "Uncle Jed said he saw you two together?"

"We're just…friends," said Thomas in a low voice.

"Just friends?" Mr. Creeper sniffed. He frowned and swiveled back to the instrument tray, selecting the trocar, a long, hollow needle. Then he bent over the corpse as Thomas looked away, squirming like a freshly caught salmon on a fish hook. Thomas hated needles and knew that he would be responsible for disinfecting the trocar after his father was done. This task—along with wiping down the counters, sweeping the floor, and cottoning down the corpse (a particularly dreadful task that involved the insertion of cotton balls into the corpse's mouth)—formed Thomas's regular "list" of duties whenever a corpse was in residence at Creeper & Sons.

"Well, I am glad to hear that," said Mr. Creeper, fitting a hose to the trocar. "These years, Elijah Thomas, are a critical stage in your apprenticeship. By your age I had already performed my first treatment and sealing of a corpse. Can you imagine that?"

Thomas couldn't. And more importantly—he didn't want to.

"This is the Creeper life, the Creeper way," Mr. Creeper continued. "Remember that well, Elijah Thomas. Friends will come and go like ships in the harbor. But family...family is the dock, my boy, steadfast and sure, keeping everything grounded amid the shifting tides."

Mr. Creeper paused and smiled, clearly pleased with his maritime analogies. "Now finish your inventory and you may be dismissed. Your mother thinks you need some...*time* to let this all set in. I know you were fond of Father Mulvaney."

Thomas nodded and set about his evening list: disinfecting the instruments, inventorying the massive jars of formaldehyde, and making sure that there were ample supplies of cotton balls, latex gloves, sanitary masks, and, of course, several tubs of bleach.

When all was tidy, Thomas removed his mask and gloves and dropped them in the garbage bin. At the door of the Preparing Room he paused and looked back at his father, whose arms moved as if in some kind of strange symphony, like a conductor, only his father's baton was a needle. Thomas could hear him as he bent over the corpse, murmuring softly as he lovingly went about his work. Thomas made sure to muffle his groan of disgust in the palm of his hand before he closed the door.

He left the Preparing Room and padded his way to the kitchen door, which was ajar.

He could see his mother inside, sitting motionless at one end of the kitchen table that had been set for the evening meal. In one hand, his mother clutched a white dinner napkin from the fourth place setting, the one she set every evening for David and cleared after the meal was done.

Thomas headed down the dark hallway to the winding staircase that rose to the turreted section of the old Victorian house. He wasn't hungry. How could anyone eat after sticking their hands in a corpse's mouth, especially somebody you'd once known? Head drooping, like an exhausted soldier returned from the brutal theater of war, he ascended the creaking staircase and went into his bedroom, closing the door behind him.

From a locked drawer in his desk, he retrieved the iPhone his parents had given David on his fifteenth birthday. The service had long since been cut off, of course, but Thomas had successfully hacked his father's Wi-Fi password and made regular use of the email app.

Two new messages from Jeni waited in his inbox—one, with the latest cipher she hoped to stump him with, and another with "*SO?????????*" in the subject line. Thomas loved anything to do with spies and code breaking and had read every book in the Gloomsbury Memorial Library about spycraft. He hoped to be a spy someday…or a writer…or a combination of both if the job existed, which he was pretty sure it didn't. Tonight, however, he didn't think that even an email with a brain-stumping cipher from Jeni could lighten his spirits. After all, it was their mutual interest in spycraft that had brought them together in the first place.

Jeni went to a private school in nearby Rhode Island called Hampswich that had a program for "accelerated students." They probably would never have met at all if it hadn't been for a book fair at Gloomsbury Memorial Library where she and Thomas had both reached for the same book, *Spies, Ciphers, and Poisoned Capsules: A C.I.A. Operative Tells All.* From that day on they became fast friends.

Thomas powered off the phone just as Moses, the family's large Maine Coon cat, pushed his way through the door and leapt onto Thomas's bed. The cat meowed plaintively until Thomas retrieved a small tin of cookies from under the bed. He fed Moses a few butter cookies and listened to the cat munching in the darkness for a while before drifting off to sleep.

Sometime in the middle of the night he awoke, shivering.

He had cracked the window open a few inches the night before, hoping to air out the smells of the musty, old house, but had forgotten to close it. His bedsheets lay in a pile on the floor next to an open—and empty—tin of cookies. *Stupid cat*, he thought, climbing out of bed and fastening the lid back on the tin. A gust of chilly wind swept through the room, rustling the curtains and raising goosebumps all across Thomas's skin. He turned to close the window. But peering out into the darkness, he froze.

Under one of the streetlamps a black car idled. Grabbing his glasses from his bedside table, Thomas peered out, over the overgrown yard swirling with fresh fog, to the street beyond. It wasn't his family's Customline hearse. This car had a long hood rounded on the sides, like the barrel of a gun, and bright headlights that lit up the pavement. A spare wheel was fastened to the side, just like a car from an old gangster film.

Three figures, clad in dark suits and wearing matching English bowler hats, were gathered around the car. (Bowler hats, in case you don't know—and Thomas certainly did—were hats with rounded sides favored by detectives like John Watson in the illustrated Sherlock Holmes mysteries Thomas loved to read.) Feeling a weird mixture of fear and excitement, Thomas leaned farther out the window, hoping to get a better look at the figures amid the swirling fog. The three men appeared to be in the middle of some intense discussion. *What on earth were they doing out there, arguing in front of his house this late at night?* Thomas wondered, wishing he could hear what they were saying. Then the thought occurred to him: The Surveille 6000, his new spy sound recorder and microphone, would be perfect for the task.

He had secretly purchased the set of spy tools online a few months before, a surprise he had hoped to share with Jeni when the summer months got boring, which they always did. The long condenser microphone could pick up sounds from over a hundred and fifty feet away…or so the manufacturer had promised.

Heart racing, he grabbed the recorder from where he had stashed it in the bottom of his sock drawer, powered it on, and positioned the long condenser mic of the Surveille 6000 on the windowsill. He pulled the headphones over his ears and listened.

The men's voices were strange—all whispery and silky, as if an orchestra of whispers had been looped through an old tape machine. The sound made the hairs on the back of Thomas's neck stand straight up. Within the strange chorus of whispers, he could distinguish a few words: *The priest…he has it…the location…he has it.*

Suddenly, one of the men detached from the group. He circled around the car and passed through the unlatched gate…heading straight for the steps to the house! Thomas gasped and nearly dropped the microphone. *What was the man doing? What could he possibly want with the Creepers?* As the man came closer, the moonlight shone through the gaps in the cypress trees above the house, illuminating the lower half of his face not hidden by the shadow of his bowler. Thomas wanted to cover his eyes. The man's skin was sickly white, paler than the moonlight, and a wicked smile played upon his pale lips. Even from such a distance, high up in his bedroom, the smile made Thomas feel horribly uneasy. The man crept closer, crossing the muddy flagstones, but after a few paces he stopped short.

A small white figure appeared on the wet flagstones, blocking his path.

The ghost-girl! Thomas realized, recognizing the small, pale silhouette.

A weird, raucous laughter erupted from the men around the car, blaring in Thomas's headphones. Advancing toward the ghost-girl, the grinning man began to slowly pull back his jacket sleeves. Thomas's eyes widened with horror. *The man's arms glowed!* They were covered were dozens of fluorescent tattoos that squirmed and writhed across the skin as if they were alive. The ghost-girl, however, to Thomas's astonishment, seemed unconcerned. Turning her head, she stared into the shadows of the overgrown bushes framing the house as the bushes started to rattle.

Out of the shadows something large but invisible, like a freak cloud of wind, burst forth. Gripping the windowsill with trembling fingers, Thomas leaned farther out to see what might cause such a disturbance. He could see large footprints in the grass—but no body making them. The men's weird laughter died in his headphones as the ghost-girl turned to face the grinning man once more. Slowly, she removed her arms from within the folds of her dress.

Thomas covered his mouth, muffling the cry before it could give him away.

One of the girl's arms was missing at the elbow, ending in a jutting white bone and a mass of red tendons. She raised her severed arm and the invisible cloud of wind started spinning around the yard like a cyclone, rattling the railings and shutters, sending a flurry of dry leaves across the pavement, and knocking the man to his knees. Clambering to his feet, he pulled down his sleeves, and the wild, writhing light disappeared. Before turning back to the car, he cast a long, lingering glance up toward Thomas's bedroom window. Thomas slunk down a few inches, gripping the microphone against his chest. His heart pounded up in his throat. When he inched back up again he could see it: the man staring up at his window! Flashing one last ghoulish grin, the man slipped out the rotting gate and climbed inside the black car waiting at the curb. The engine revved like the throaty growl of a wild animal, then peeled off into the fog, its two red taillights trailing down the block.

The Creeper Family Diary

II

The Creeper Family Diary

Thomas awoke to the sound of footsteps in the downstairs foyer.

An old dumbwaiter shaft went from his bedroom to the small kitchen off the foyer, and it was a peculiar quirk of his room that he could hear just about everything that went on in the foyer two floors below. (A dumbwaiter, just in case you didn't know, is not an ignorant person working in a restaurant, but a moveable shelf-pulley system that allows you to move plates of food from the kitchen to rooms upstairs.)

Rubbing his eyes, he rolled over halfway in bed. He reached over, feeling blindly for his glasses on his side table. He slipped the glasses over the bridge of his nose and blinked a few times. The Surveille 6000 lay on the dusty floorboards next to the window. The sight of the spy device made him bolt upright in bed, throwing off his covers as the events of the previous night came flooding back to him: the strange antique car and its even stranger occupants; the man with the glowing arms; the ghost-girl; the invisible cyclone that seemed to sweep up out of nowhere and throw the man backwards as if he weighed nothing at all. He could remember lying down on the bed after it all happened, closing his eyes tight and wanting to get lost in that darkness—forget that he had seen the man grinning up at his window. He must have fallen asleep trying to wish away the horrible nightmare he knew in his heart had been real.

The creaking footsteps brought him back to the present.

Leaping out of bed, he threw open the door and ran to

the second-floor landing. Gripping the railing, he peered down fearfully below, expecting to see a group of men in dark suits and hats led by the grinning man with fluorescent tattoos. But instead, he beheld a very different sight.

His father—recognizable by the shock of thick black hair that covered his head—was standing in the foyer shaking hands with a man…a man in a hat! It wasn't a black bowler but a large, gray floppy hat with fresh raindrops beaded across the brim like jewels. Removing the hat and his raincoat, the unknown visitor hung the items on a coatrack in the foyer and followed Thomas's father into the Funeral Director's Study.

It wasn't at all strange to have a visitor that early in the day, Thomas mused. After all, people dropped dead at all hours, day and night. He had become accustomed to relatives of the deceased coming and going, just as his mother and father had become accustomed to sleeping in their clothes in the event of a knock at the funeral door. But as he slipped back into his room, Thomas had his first real shock of the morning:

The ghost-girl stood by his dresser, her arms once again folded behind her back, her pale face gazing up at him with the same plaintive, mute stare.

"W-w-what…" Thomas began but then stopped and swallowed hard, trying to steady the quiver in his voice. "What do you want?" The girl turned her head, fixing her eyes upon Thomas's bookshelf. "A book?" said Thomas. "Is that it? That's what you've been looking for all this time?"

He sprang to the bookshelf like a cat, eager to find anything that might send the ghost away, even if she was responsible for protecting the house from the man with the glowing tattoos from the previous night. He scanned the titles in his collection—books about spies, a few animes…a couple of textbooks, including a copy of *Embalming: History, Theory, and Practice* still in its shrink-wrap. *What could she want with any of them?* he wondered. "Wait! You're not looking for a book…

are you?" he said slowly, the threads of the mystery starting to unweave in his mind. "It's something else in here, right?"

The girl nodded.

"Something to do with the bookshelf," Thomas whispered to himself. Like all the other dilapidated and musty furniture in the house, the bookshelf in Thomas's room had stood against that same wall for hundreds of years, one of many antiques passed down through the Creeper family line. Positioning his shoulder against one side of the bookcase, he dug in and pushed with all his strength, his feet slipping on the wooden floor. The bookcase groaned and shifted, scattering dust motes into the air. Another push and the bookcase slid a few more feet. Thomas's jaw dropped. The light shining from his desk lamp revealed a rectangular outline in the wall. A secret door!

There was no doorknob or handle left, just a small hole the size of nickel drilled into the wood. Thomas stuck his finger into the hole and pulled. The door cracked open. He held his breath. The dark, recessed space within resembled a small closet, approximately the size of Thomas's bathroom. The secret room was dominated by a standing bassinet, fringed in black lace and laden with a thick film of dust. Wedging the door a bit wider, Thomas could see toys that must have belonged to a child once—a little toy shaker with a rusted bell, a teddy bear with one of its eyes missing, and, in the moldy bedding of the bassinet, a small book. *A book*....

Thomas turned around. But the ghost-girl was already at his elbow. The death chill wafted over her, as if she contained all the frost of the Arctic in her bones. With a trembling hand, Thomas pulled the book from the bassinet. Brushing off the dust, he could make out a name inscribed in gold leaf in the cracked black leather. *Silvie.*

"Silvie?" Thomas asked. "Is that you?"

The ghost-girl nodded.

Opening the book, a whiff of mildew, dust, and old parchment filled his nostrils. He buried his nose and coughed into his shirt. It seemed as if the book had not been read for quite some time. As he leafed carefully through the pages, something slipped to the floor. Reaching down with a trembling hand, Thomas retrieved it and held it up to his glasses.

It was a slender sheaf of pages, yellowed and cracked at the edges. Unfolding the pages, he immediately recognized the stamped seal at the bottom—the large *C* with the wreathed insignia of the Creeper family. The pages had been cut from the Creeper family diary!

Returning to his bed, he quickly read the first page, the chill of the ghost-girl prickling his neck as she hovered close behind his ear.

> 3 March 1927
> Tragedy befalls our house! Our darling Silvie was laid to rest this morning. Arthur killed the beast who took our angel's arm. How can an animal that was once so sweet and docile have become so malicious and deranged? We shall never recover from this dreadful affliction. All Souls above hear my solemn prayer: may my sweet Silvie never leave my side. May she know, even in the shade beyond this world, that her mother is close and that she loves her eternally.

"A beast did this to you?" said Thomas. Silvie shook her head. "I…I don't understand," said Thomas. "It says—"

He was poisoned! The magician tried to use him for his act but the magic poisoned him!

Fingal would never hurt a fly!

The words reverberated through his head like a loud speaker. But they weren't his own words, nor his own voice. It was a young girl's voice. She was somehow communicating with him inside his own skull! He gaped in wonder at the sheer impossibility of it all.

"How did you do that?" Thomas stammered after he found his breath again. "Speak inside my head like that?"

You found my Artifact of Unlocking, dumb-dumb! Every spirit that can't go on to the next place has an Artifact of Unlocking. Once you find a spirit's Artifact, they can talk to you. Well, most of them… some are just angry and like to scream a lot.

Thomas sank to the edge of his bed. It was one thing to be haunted by the girl. Now he could hear her inside his brain. Even though he wanted to hear her story, he wasn't sure how he felt about this new development in their relationship.

"What was that thing in the bushes last night?" he asked. "It was like some kind of wind storm that came out of nowhere."

That's Fingal, my puppy. The magician gave him secret powers but the powers changed him and drove him mad. That's why he took my arm. Thomas, you have to help me find my arm. If you help us, Fingal and I will help protect you from them.

Thomas's blood froze.

He thought of the grinning man with the fluorescent tattoos and shuddered. It was as if he were locked in a movie theater, forced to watch the same terrifying reel over and over again of that man, that face…that sickly, pale face staring up at him through the fog.

"You know who they are?" he said, his voice weak as a mouse's whisper. "I mean…you've seen them before?"

Silvie nodded.

Only once…a long time ago. I was walking down Town Beach with my mother, when I saw one of them on the rocks at the edge of the water. He took a pair of glasses from his pocket and when he put them on, he disappeared! It's how they move around when no one's paying attention. They think that your friend the priest found out about them...found out what can hurt them. They'll never leave you alone now, Thomas, not until they get what they want.

"Get what they want?" Thomas shouted, rushing to the window. He glanced around frantically. But there was no black car idling beyond the rotting fence, no wild and swirling fog. "What the hell does any of this have to do with me?" he barked over his shoulder.

He saw you, Thomas, looking down at him from the window. He knows you know about them now!

"I don't know anything about them," Thomas yelled. He turned away from the window and covered his face in his hands. "I'm sorry," he murmured through the cracks in his fingers. "It's just...I don't understand why all this is happening."

I know, but you can't run away, not from this kind of trouble, Thomas. Fingal and I will help you. Do you want our help or not?

"Fine," said Thomas. "I mean, yes, thank you." He thought about Jeni. What would Jeni do at the beginning of a mystery? She would find out what a killer or a thief wanted—their motive. "I need to figure out who these guys are," he said, with renewed determination. "Why they're in Gloomsbury. How we can—*if* we can make them leave. After we figure that out—"

Then you'll help me find my arm?

"Yes," said Thomas, smiling at the ghost-girl's persistence. "Then I'll help you find your arm."

Great! Then I better tell you my full name! Once you know a spirit's name you are joined together in the Bond.

"Super," Thomas muttered under his breath.

Don't be a jerk! My name is Silvie Creeper. I'm your great aunt or something. Fingal is sleeping outside right now. You'll meet him later. He doesn't get up until the moon is out. He's pretty superstitious.

Thomas smiled. *A superstitious ghost-dog with magical powers?* Now he had heard everything. He checked his Ken Darby Spy Watch. It was almost half past eleven. He was supposed to meet Jeni at Sal's in thirty minutes. He couldn't believe he'd slept so late. His father would be furious.

"I gotta go, Silvie," said Thomas. "I'll let you know what I find out."

Silvie nodded. A small smile, something he had never seen in all the encounters with the ghost-girl, flashed over her pale face.

"One more thing," said Thomas, blushing and staring

back down at the ground. "You can't see me…like *all* the time, right? Like in the shower?"

But when he looked up the ghost was gone.

❧

Thomas knocked on the door of his father's study.

"Enter!" bellowed Elijah Creeper the Fifth.

Thomas pushed back the creaking door. Under the soft light cast by a few dusty sconces, he could see his father across the room, sitting in a large wingback chair behind a massive jet-black desk the size of a small boat. Visibly annoyed by the intrusion, Elijah Creeper the Fifth peered sternly back at Thomas over the top of his gold-rimmed glasses, his long bony fingers folded together on the desktop. In the chair across from his father, Thomas could see the top half of the visitor's head. The head was closely shaved, revealing a pale scalp. One gloved hand was raised in the air above the arm of the visitor's chair, and he seemed to have been conducting a lively conversation with Thomas's father before Thomas's arrival. On the wood-paneled walls on either side of the massive desk, looming like religious icons, were the portraits of Thomas's ancestors, The Elijahs.

Thomas had never been able to look The Elijahs directly in the eyes. He swore, though he could never prove it, that their expressions changed from week to week. It didn't help that all of them—every single male ancestor who had taken over command of Creeper & Sons—had either died or vanished as a whiff of smoke vanishes after a match is extinguished.

There was Elijah Creeper the First, with his egg-shaped bald head and pencil-thin moustache, who had disappeared in the night, leaving behind a note in his scrawled shorthand with one word on its face—*Worms*; Elijah Creeper the Second, with his walrus-like muttonchops and lazy eye, framed by a monocle. He had gone mad from formaldehyde fumes, filled his bathrobe with rocks, and walked into the ocean in the middle of February. Then there was Elijah Creeper the Third, who looked perpetually stunned, as if having just swallowed a razor blade. He met his end after inexplicably shoving his arms into a shark cannery grinder, claiming that it was the only way to get rid of the "infernal itching in his palms." Needless to say, he was pulled head first into the deadly machine.

Finally, there was Thomas's grandfather, Elijah Creeper the Fourth, a cruel taskmaster who administered lessons in the Preparing Room using a riding crop to wallop his two sons whenever they were too slow to respond.

Those sons—Elijah Creeper the Fifth, Thomas's father, and Jedediah Creeper, Thomas's uncle (whom everyone called Jed)—had clearly had a rough upbringing, explaining perhaps their differently twisted, but equally unsympathetic lives. Elijah Creeper the Fourth would die in a freak accident during Gloomsbury's first (and last) Fourth of July parade. *The Gloomsbury Morning Chronicle* described the incident in grim detail. Horrified onlookers were said to have seen a deranged horse with "wild blue fire spurting from its eyes" break free of its reins and trample Elijah Creeper the Fourth into hoof-marked pâté. While Thomas felt sorry for anyone meeting such a horrible end, the irony of the situation did not escape him—a man who used a riding crop to drive home his lessons and orders, met his own gruesome death beneath the flailing hooves of a possessed horse.

His father's voice, crackling like lightning out of the gloom, startled Thomas from the dark train of his thoughts. "How good of you to rise from your slumbers!" exclaimed Elijah Creeper the Fifth, his voice laden with venomous sarcasm. "Elijah Thomas, this is Mr. Richie Mulvaney, Father Mulvaney's nephew."

A square-jawed man in his mid-thirties swung around in his chair to face Thomas. He had a blond beard as thick and curly as a sheepskin coat and stained yellow teeth, which he bared in a smile. The man's skin was so pale, even by

Gloomsbury standards, that at first sight Thomas thought the man an albino.

"So this is the boy!" Richie exclaimed, extending his hand, which Thomas reluctantly took, feeling the eyes of Elijah Creeper the Fifth—indeed, the eyes of *all* the Elijahs in the room—bearing down on him.

Thomas discovered the man's fingers to be cold and clammy. He released the hand as quickly as he could without being impolite.

"What a treat to meet the heir of this great household," Richie said. "It's quite a time capsule, I must say. Your father was just giving me a little history lesson before you came in."

There was an awkward pause, as if Richie were awaiting Thomas's response. Richie Mulvaney's dark eyes roved over him, as if sizing up tailoring measurements for a suit. His stare made Thomas feel uneasy.

"Yes, yes, what do you want, Elijah Thomas?" Elijah Creeper the Fifth snapped impatiently.

Thomas made sure the lie was airtight in his brain before he uttered it aloud. There was no way his father would let him meet Jeni for pizza. But because his parents had decided his homeschooling would start in the fall—that being the best way to transition to full-time funeral home duties—Thomas had a secret card to play, and he would play it until the game was up: the library.

"I was hoping to get a jumpstart on my studies," he said. "I'd like to go to the library for a few hours, if that's all right."

"Excellent!" beamed Elijah Creeper the Fifth. "Indeed, you will want to be fully prepared for next year. You have a great deal to learn—biological systems, the fluid mechanics of this arterial masterpiece we call the body! Be back in time for the dressing. We've received a number of items this morning the family wishes Father Mulvaney be interred with. Your cousin George sent them, I believe?" Mr. Creeper continued, turning to Richie. "We spoke on the phone earlier this morning."

For a few moments another awkward silence reigned in the study, and Thomas turned to find Richie Mulvaney again staring at him with the same scrutinizing, inscrutable look as before. He may have been Pop's nephew, but Thomas couldn't remember ever seeing him around St. Mary's and certainly Pop had never mentioned him.

"Yes, of course," Richie finally said, nodding back at Mr. Creeper. "Cousin George. Always so thoughtful."

Seizing the opportunity to excuse himself, Thomas slipped out of the dark study, trying not to appear too elated—for while libraries are indeed wonderful places, they never compare to a hot meal shared in secret with a best friend.

As the door closed behind him, Thomas could hear his father apologizing for his son's "lack of social graces." Gritting his teeth, Thomas crossed the foyer and stepped out onto the porch.

"Hullo, Tommy boy!" a deep voice rumbled up from the shadows of a rotting archway.

Thomas didn't need to turn around to know that Uncle Jed was lounging against the side of the porch. Stale cigarette smoke hung in the air, combined with the familiar aroma of scotch and cheap aftershave.

"Whaddya think happened here last night?" said Uncle Jed, pointing toward the strange divots across the yard. "Looks like Gloomsbury High's football team ran a training camp in the yard, huh?"

Thomas peered up at his uncle. Of the two sons born into the last generation of the Creeper family, Jedidiah Creeper had taken the lion's share of bad luck. Having had enough of the relentless cracking of Elijah the Fourth's riding crop, he jumped ship for a tour of duty in Vietnam that left half his face disfigured from a napalm explosion outside the fallen city of Saigon.

Uncle Jed concealed his scars with a partial mask that covered the left side of his face, just like the Phantom of the Opera. Sometimes for fun, or just to speed up the line at the grocery store, he would tip the mask back and giggle at the poor soul's discomfort. He wore the same outfit, night or day, a greasy green army jacket that was all threadbare at the elbows and covered with patches that proclaimed "P.O.W.," "Ditch Nixon!" along with a few patches indicating the Fraternal Order of New England Longshoremen which Thomas assumed his uncle had stolen in order to gain entrance to the Longshoremen's pub where drinks were half-priced for all fraternal "brothers" bearing the patch.

Thomas's father would have fired Jed long ago from the family business if not for a clause in Elijah the Fourth's will that stated in clear, unswerving language:

All immediate members of the Creeper family are to be employed exclusively and without exception in the family business until they are no longer physically capable.

The "physically capable" was often a bone of contention with Uncle Jed.

He managed the pickups between Gloomsbury's small morgue and the funeral home, though it was arguable that he picked up more speeding tickets than corpses due to his lead foot. There were also the times—after one too many scotches at the Longshoremen's pub or at Sappy's Diner on Weiland Avenue, which became a bar after five o'clock—that a body would be forgotten in the back seat until the following morning.

Thomas rapidly descended the porch steps, trying his best to ignore Uncle Jed's cackling behind him. "It's okay, Tommy boy! No need to get all bent out of shape! You don't think I've seen strange things around this house! Maybe we'll talk about it someday, eh? Some other time?"

Thomas glanced over his shoulder. His uncle leered back at him, cleaning his nails with the toothpick from the Swiss army knife he always carried in his coat pocket. Uncle Jed made a couple of "Ooooh oooooh ooooh!" ghost sounds, then let out another wicked cackle. Thomas shook his head and kept on walking.

Ten minutes later he arrived at the stained red-white-and-green awning of Sal's Pizzeria just in time to see Jeni and her younger brother Arnold round the corner of the street, arguing at the top of their lungs.

"I told you not to go in there!" yelled Arnold, stabbing his finger at Jeni's face. "If Mom and Dad find out I've been getting packages from Captain Sparky's—"

"Oh, shut up!" Jeni snapped, cutting him off. Her expression of complete and utter irritation dissolved as soon as she saw Thomas standing at the door of the pizzeria. "Hey, Thomas!" she shouted.

"What is he doing here?" asked Thomas.

"I know, I know," said Jeni, throwing up her hands. "He caught me going through his secret stash. Not so secret now, huh, *Arn-hole*?"

"Don't call me that!" Arnold shouted back.

Exasperated, Jeni blew a few strands of hair out of her eyes. "Whatever! He said he'd tell my parents about me skipping soccer last week to go the movies if I didn't buy him a pizza."

"Hey, Creepy Thomas," said Arnold, grinning a gummy smile through a mouthful of steel braces. "Seen any dead people lately?"

Jeni elbowed him in the stomach. Arnold let out a loud *omph!* "Hey!" Arnold protested. "I didn't come up with the name! Everybody calls him that—"

"Move it, *Arn-hole*, go figure out what you want to eat," said Jeni, hauling Arnold up the steps. "I'm sorry, Thomas." Arnold made a "braceful exit"—sneering at Jeni and Thomas with his giant mechanical chompers—before slipping into the pizzeria alive with sounds of guests chattering and the chefs yelling, "Order up!" Once he was gone, Jeni pulled Thomas out of the rain and under the awning.

"So..." she said. "Did you break my cipher yet?"

"Almost," Thomas lied. "It's a real good one, Jen. Hey, can we go in?"

"Why?" said Jeni. "You starving or something, professor?

"No," said Thomas. "I just don't want Arnold setting fire to anything. Couldn't imagine the only good place to eat in Gloomsbury going up in flames. Do your parents just hide all the matches and lighters in the house?"

"Something like that," said Jeni, smiling as they stepped into the lively restaurant.

Inside, they found Arnold waiting in a booth, drumming his fingers against the clear tabletop with local ads for Gloomsbury businesses plastered beneath. A large ad for Archibald Tanners showed a couple of Gloomsbury locals having just emerged from the tanning booths, but because of the intense pallor of their skin, the "bronzing" process had turned them the orange color of Oompa-Loompas from *Charlie and the Chocolate Factory*. Thomas and Jeni slid into the booth. After a minute, during which Jeni forced a packet of complimentary restaurant matches out of Arnold's vise-like grip, the waitress came to take their order. No surprise, Arnold ordered the Upper-Decker Philly Steak n' Cheese Triple Stuffer, complete with three types of cheese stuffed into the crust, which was, of course, the most expensive item on the menu.

Twenty minutes later—after Arnold had told them, in excruciating detail, about how he was going to blow up his collection of Ninjagos with military-grade dynamite ("I wanna see how their heads fly!")—the waitress returned with the steaming pizza. As soon as the proper amount of time passed for cooling (ten seconds), Arnold laid into the pie like a sailor returned from months at sea who'd survived on sardines and greased deck shavings. Coming up for a rare breath of air, he grinned at Thomas, a disgusting mosaic of steak and pizza entangled in his jagged braces.

Once he had cleaned his plate, Arnold belched noxious pizza fumes and slipped out of the booth, heading over to chat with friends from school he'd spied at another table.

"I've so many things to tell you, Jen," said Thomas once

he was sure Arnold was out of earshot. "You're not gonna believe it."

Jeni flashed her usual wry smile and flipped her hair back over her ears. "Try me."

Thomas decided that he'd leave out the part about Silvie and Fingal, the poisoned magical ghost-dog, since he knew Jeni didn't believe in ghosts. He told her instead about the antique car and the strange figures outside his house the previous night, their whispery references to a priest knowing the location. With a shudder, he told her about the grinning man with the swirling, glowing tattoos, how he started toward the house and caught Thomas looking down from his window. Eyes wide, Jeni slouched farther into the booth, a stunned expression on her face. A finger under her chin—her classic thinking pose—she murmured, "Coincidence?"—more to herself, it seemed, than to Thomas.

"What did you say?" said Thomas.

Jeni squinted. Whenever she was working out some great riddle or code, she made a certain kind of face, as if she were forcing laser beams from her eyes like Cyclops in *X-Men* but wasn't having any luck.

"It can't be a coincidence...right?" she whispered. They sat in silence for a few moments, broken here and there by the three chefs behind the counter whirling disks of dough in the air and shouting in Italian. They all wore the same matching green, white, and red chef coats, and created quite a show, which was half the fun of going to Sal's. But this afternoon, Thomas and Jeni had other things on their minds.

"I've got it!" Jeni suddenly exclaimed. "I bet Pop Mulvaney figured out who these psychos are. He must have discovered something...something he knew could hurt them! And what if...what if they killed him before he could find it or reveal what he knew to someone else? All I know is these weird guys hanging around and Pop dying can't be a coincidence. Remember that line from *Spies, Ciphers, and Poisoned Capsules*? 'A good spy or detective doesn't believe in coincidence.' The only thing I can't figure out is those swirling tattoos. Are you sure you didn't just hit your head or something?"

"Yeah, I'm sure," said Thomas tightly.

"Hey! Hey! I believe you, professor!" said Jeni. "Don't go all tweaky on me."

Jeni reached across the table and covered Thomas's hand with her own. They both looked at it for a second before Jeni hastily removed her hand.

"Here's what I figure we need to do," she said. "I say we go—"

Suddenly, a large piece of pizza, dripping with melted cheese, sailed across the room and landed in Jeni's Pepsi, toppling her glass and spilling soda all down the front of her shorts.

Thomas's face went white.

Jeni's face went red.

"Jeni...don't..." Thomas began.

But it was too late.

Jeni Myers leapt up from the booth like a cat pouncing on a fleeing mouse. She crossed the room to where Arnold sat giggling with several other boys, including, Thomas saw, someone he didn't care to ever see again. Not a ghost. Ghosts he could handle.

It was Gary Korvin.

"Listen to me, you freakin' dung beetles!" Jeni yelled. "Arnold! Go back to your seat!"

The voice was so powerful, so filled with impressive authority, that even one of the chefs tossing dough behind the counter lost his rhythm, sending the pie a little too high in the air to where it stuck to the underside of the fan whirling overhead.

Arnold giggled again, not budging an inch.

Bad move, thought Thomas, wincing. *Bad move.*

Like an insane mama cat, Jeni grabbed Arnold by the collar and swung him up onto his feet.

"Okay, okay!" cried Arnold. "Relax!"

Now Jeni set her burning sights on her next victim.

"Gary Korvin, I should expect this much from someone who's been kicked off the football team two years in a row! The next time you mess with me or my friend Thomas I'll make sure everyone at school knows I watched your dad spank you over the hood of his BMW last summer! *Spank* you, Gary. Got that image? Does everybody have that image firmly planted in their heads?"

Jeni looked around the room at the patrons whose side conversations had been instantly silenced by the unbridled force of Jeni Myers. An old lady in a hairnet, sipping hot lemon tea, made a shocked *O* with her mouth that looked as if she might have just swallowed an entire lemon. Gary Korvin, who had a word for everything at any time—all of them horrible—was, for the first time in his life, rendered utterly speechless.

Jeni returned to the table, Arnold trailing behind her, trying to look like he hadn't just been completely outmatched by his sister.

Without missing a beat, Jeni went back to her pizza while Thomas stared back in awe.

"What?" Jeni said after a few bites.

"That was…kind of raw, Jen," said Thomas though he couldn't help but crack a smile. Man, was he glad to have Jeni Myers on his side.

"Later, losers," Arnold mumbled and rose from the table. He made one last scowl in Thomas's direction before heading out the door and disappearing into the rain-swept street.

"He's not that bad, you know," said Jeni after a few more bites.

"Gary or Arnold?" said Thomas.

"Arnold, silly," said Jeni. "Yeah, he's an idiot most of the time. But I think he just puts it on to impress people like Gary Korvin. Why do you think Gary hates you so much, by the way?"

Thomas looked across the room. Gary was thumbing the

blade of a butter knife while looking intently at Thomas. Thomas shook his head.

"He's a cousin of the Sneeds," said Thomas. "All the Sneeds hate the Creepers for something that happened, like, a *bajillion* years ago. My dad won't even talk about it. But apparently, the feud is still so bad that when a Sneed family member dies, they take the body to Marvale to get prepared and then bring it back to Gloomsbury to be buried."

"Wow, that is bad," said Jeni, arching her eyebrows. "Hey, you still up for going to the library?"

"I kind of have to," said Thomas. "I told my dad I was getting a start on my studies for next year.'" Jeni almost spit out her pizza crust. "What? What's so funny?" Thomas asked, smiling at the sound of Jeni's true laugh—not her sarcastic scoff that she made most of the time—but the rare, giggly-down-to-your bones laugh of pure joy Thomas loved.

"It's just that you're such a horrible liar, Thomas Creeper," said Jeni, pushing her plate away from her. She removed a small wallet from her sweatshirt pocket.

Thomas's jaw dropped.

He could see the image of Arnold Myers's face on a card fit into the clear outside pocket. It was a member card for Captain Sparky's Firework Emporium Frequent Buyers Club. Jeni lifted the crisp twenty-dollar bill from the folds of the wallet.

"You didn't!" Thomas whispered.

"He's got to save his allowance for things other than fireworks, right?" said Jeni. "Those are my parents' words, not mine."

Thomas was flabbergasted. Jeni Myers was not from this planet.

"C'mon, professor," said Jeni, sliding out of the booth. "Let's go get a head start on your studies."

❧

Halfway down the block, Thomas stopped, pulling Jeni

behind him into the open gate of Ms. Trautwein's overgrown vegetable garden.

"It's them, Jen!" he exclaimed in a choked voice. "Look! It's the car from last night, I'm sure of it!"

Up ahead, they could see a sleek, black antique car with a wheel on its side rolling slowly down the block. The car moved slowly, like a predator, as if whoever was inside was scanning the block looking for someone. The windows of the car were tinted black, but Jeni could see a faint fluorescent glow behind the windows.

"God, I wish you had hit your head," Jeni whispered.

Thomas cast Jeni an incredulous sideways look.

"You know what I mean," said Jeni. "You're right. Something weird *is* going on. Let's go the back way to the library. Okay?"

Thomas nodded. For once, all the Gary Korvins and the bitter Sneeds of the world seemed like jokes, like nonexistent threats. There was something far more sinister and terrifying living within Gloomsbury, moving through its streets, right under everyone's nose.

And he and Jeni were the only ones who knew it.

Ethel Sneed

III

Ms. Katz Pulls a Black and White Photograph

There were few spots in town where Thomas could go without being reminded that he was different from other kids his age, that he was a soon-to-be homeschooled mortician's apprentice who touched dead people on a regular basis. The library was one of those rare havens. Its deep stacks and cloistered reading nooks provided a refuge for Thomas when the shadow of his life turned a shade more miserable.

Once a hospital for sailors who'd spent too much time at sea, Gloomsbury Memorial Library had become the pet project of Ethel Sneed—grandmother of the town's current wealthy recluse, J.W. Sneed—during the early 1900s. Blind in one eye, but refusing to wear an eye patch, Eagle-Eyed Ethel once ruled the checkout counter with one working eye and two iron fists. Though barely five feet tall, she commanded a presence that ensured children returned books on time, fearing to incur the "Wrath of Sneed"—a relentless stream of vituperative and threatening notes, each one emblazoned with the letter *S* in a pressed wax seal upon the envelope.

An outbreak of lethal mold in the late 1980s devastated half of the library's holdings, including (to the great relief of the residents of Gloomsbury) the giant portrait of Eagle-Eyed Ethel that had once hung in the library's foyer like a salute to a cruel and merciless dictator.

But if Ethel Sneed and her two daughters, Gretta and Grava—who took up their mother's form of militant library science after her death—were examples of nasty, crooked people who had no business being around children, then Eloise Katz, the current town librarian, was the complete opposite.

Ms. Katz, or Ms. K. as she was lovingly known around the library, was the first to institute an "on your honor" program with book lending that worked just as well, if not better, than a pen-and-ink threat from a wicked Sneed. She replaced the dull, mold-ridden tapestries in the hallway, depicting horrible shark attacks and gloomy mist-shrouded cemeteries, with an installation celebrating human innovation throughout the centuries. Lastly—perhaps Ms. Katz's greatest coup to date—she employed bright young people as "pages," an old term for library assistant. Other employment prospects for young people in Gloomsbury were not promising: there was the pungent job of sludge collection and jellyfish removal at Town Beach, supervised by the stone-faced Mr. Contenescu; and there was sinkhole detection, under the sharp of eye of Mayor Plugg's strong man, Bruno Bulger, who kept a safe distance while children tiptoed around the edges of suspected sinkholes to detect "cracking points." Each year a Processing Scholarship was awarded by the Sneed Foundation, who pre-selected one "lucky" person to be shown the ropes at the Sneed Waste Removal Factory, which was filled with so many cameras (due to the family's paranoia) that Processing Scholars felt as if they were working in a sewage internment camp. Needless to say, all kids in town hoping for a little padding to their weekly allowances clamored for work from Ms. K.

"Hiya, bookworms!" Ms. Katz called out as Thomas and Jeni walked through the library's large revolving door. In a gap between a pyramid of recently returned books, they spotted the cheerful, bespectacled face of their favorite librarian. Because Gloomsbury had less resources than other nearby towns like Hampswich—which boasted a state-of-the-art library with a 3D hologram display of the Founding

Fathers—librarians like Ms. Katz had to make do with the bare minimum. All the more reason why Thomas and Jeni loved to help her any chance they could.

Thomas and Jeni waved to Ms. K and headed down into the library stacks. When they reached the nonfiction side of the library Jeni paused. "Okay," she said. "Let's split up. I'll look for books on tattoos. You go see if you can find anything on that model of car. Deal?"

"Deal," said Thomas brightening a little. The world felt weird and topsy-turvy, but being with Jeni put all that weirdness at bay. He stared at Jeni for a few moments but didn't realize he was staring until Jeni laughed and pushed him playfully a few steps down the aisle. "Hop to, professor!" she chided. "And don't forget to get some books for your *studies*." She let out a giggle and disappeared down the side of another stack.

Thomas set to work. Jeni was right. He had to remember to grab a few books to fool his parents. On the shelf of the Life Sciences section, he found *Biology Today*, a massive primer on biology. He didn't need to check the inside slip to know that it had never been checked out. He pulled a copy of *The Scientific Method and You* from another shelf, and a book entitled *H.P. Korvac's Magical Emporium*, which had been wedged sideways into the stacks, making Thomas think that maybe it wasn't supposed to be there. The cover of the book featured a large lidless eye set inside a pyramid. Looking at the cover gave him a weird tingling sensation that rippled up his spine. *Who knew what interesting things the book had to say?* Tucking the book under his arm, he kept moving down the stack, until he came to the section on automobiles. But as he started to thumb the waxy plastic binding of a book entitled *The Racing Life*, he stopped.

He could hear voices coming from the other side of the stacks. One of them he recognized as Jeni's, but her voice sounded funny, as if she were reading from a script for a character in a movie.

Thomas parted a few books and looked through to the adjacent aisle.

It was Jeni.

"That's *so* ultra," said Jeni, looking up at a girl with large hooped earrings and shiny bangs that almost covered her eyes.

"That's what I told, *Ma-ri-sa!*" the girl said in a lilting voice. "We're getting the sauna put into the gym. I can't wait, Jennifer. There's gonna be skin peels and everything. It's so ultra."

Jennifer? Thomas frowned. Nobody called Jeni that. Not even her own parents when she was in trouble.

Jeni said goodbye to the girl and headed past her down the stacks. Thomas stood dumbstruck for a few moments, holding on to the side of the library shelf as a series of troubling questions circled around his brain. *Did he really know Jeni Myers? Were they really best friends if she lived a secret life where she acted like a completely different person?*

Thomas found her a few minutes later at a reading table over near the periodicals. Three or four books were propped up on the table, and Jeni's nose was buried deep in one of them. She was so engrossed in her reading that she didn't even look up from her book as Thomas approached the table and pulled out a chair.

He dropped the books on the table like a pallet full of bricks.

Jeni looked up and flashed him a nasty look.

"What the hell, Thomas?" she snarled.

"Whoops, sorry," said Thomas with fabricated sincerity. "Must have just slipped."

He stared at her for a few seconds. He was about to question the whole conversation in the stacks, but decided against it. After all, Jeni was helping *him* out, she was being a real friend, right? Helping him untangle a great mystery, even if a new mystery—the secret double life of Jenalyn Myers—had yet to be fully illuminated.

Jeni held the nasty look for another second before returning to her reading. Thomas let out a loud sigh and cracked open the first book at the top of his stack—*Automotive Treasures: A Short Visual History*. He *thwapped* through each page, glancing up to see if Jeni was watching. But if his actions annoyed her, she gave no indication of it. Her lips moved with each word she read on the page, and the only time she paused was to pull a rubber band from her wrist to tie back her long strawberry-blonde hair.

Now there was a secret skill Thomas possessed, one that not even Jeni was aware of. His talent came in handy for tests at school, or, even worse, a pop quiz by his father in the Preparing Room.

Thomas Creeper possessed a photographic memory.

It wasn't as superhuman as they make it out in movies, but it was real and powerful all the same. He could see something once, an image or a phrase, and if the material resonated with him—if he got that special tingle that felt like a ghost raising the hairs on the back of his neck, only in a positive way, like an exciting magnetic buzz—he could store the material in a secret library deep within his mind. There were days when his thoughts were too shadowy, too clouded with the misery of the funeral home for this skill to be effective. But on clear-headed days, like a rare Gloomsbury sun sighting, he could summon the knowledge to help him navigate a new situation or open a new door of thought in his mind.

As he flipped through the library book—a history of American automobiles beginning with Ford's Model T—he felt no special tingle run up his spine. There were roadsters from the 1930s and 40s, with an old black-and-white photograph of the car that the gangster John Dillinger reputedly used to escape from prison. One page featured a low-slung black car that once belonged to Al Capone. But none of these models looked much like the black car that had idled under the lamplight outside his house like some sleek, predatory creature that exhaled fog instead of exhaust.

"Any of these look familiar?" Jeni piped up, sliding *The Mark of the High Seas* across the table, opened halfway to a series of drawings. The book detailed the evolution of tattoos and tattoo artists from the earliest days of pirates and merchant sailors. He scanned the sketches and photographs of ornately drawn swallows (symbolizing the return journey, the nautical star for true north), anchors for holding fast in the storm, mermaids, and curvy women with names like Ol' Red, Black-Eyed Sue, and Lady Luck. But nowhere did Thomas see anything remotely like the markings he remembered on the grinning man's arms, swirling with fluorescent light.

"Nope," he said, sliding the book back to Jeni.

For the hundredth time, he replayed the events of that night in his mind, like a looping film he couldn't turn off—the man with the black bowler, his rolled-up sleeves and glowing arms; the whispering chorus of voices from his companions standing around the mysterious car; Silvie appearing out of nowhere and blocking his path, and the strange way in which the man had stared up at Thomas's window, as if the man had recognized him from somewhere. *Yet how could that be?* Thomas wondered. *What was he missing?*

While Jeni re-shelved the books, Thomas checked out his books from Ms. Katz's assistant, a retired volunteer named Ms. Vaughn who wore funny rose-tinted glasses and sported a large beehive hairdo that must have been popular when she was a young woman forty years before. Once the books were all stamped with their due dates, Thomas headed down the hallway toward the foyer, intending to get a drink of water from the fountain before they left.

Halfway down the hallway he stopped dead in his tracks.

"Jeni!" he hollered over his shoulder. "Over here!"

"What is it?" Jeni asked breathlessly, rushing to his side.

"In the picture! Look!" Thomas whispered, pointing at the display case with a trembling finger. "It's him, Jen…I'm sure of it."

A series of black-and-white photographs set in poster

board hung above the drinking fountain. The photographs featured views of Gloomsbury through the different eras in the town's history. In sloping black calligraphy Thomas instantly recognized as Ms. Katz's handwriting, the following words were inscribed: "*Gloomsbury: Then and Now.*" The project, completed by the Gloomsbury Historical Society and spearheaded by Ms. Katz, compared views of Gloomsbury's dockyards and beaches as they'd appeared at the turn of the century with present-day images representing the same views. Much about the town seemed unchanged over the decades: the gloom, the gray, the rust, the rain. But in some places you could see the disappearance of timely landmarks: the great Ferris Wheel on Town Beach, for instance, appeared in one photograph thronged with customers, but in the next photo, twenty years later, the Ferris Wheel had been reduced to a single rusted beam webbed with discarded fishing nets.

Thomas had passed the display a thousand times before, never paying it much mind. That morning, however, one image of dockworkers on a ship caught his eye. One man mended a fishing net, while another gutted fish; the shadow of a third tied down the mainsail. But this time, as Thomas leaned down to take a sip of water, he saw a fourth man in the photograph.

He was standing in the shadows, half hidden behind a large stack of barrels. He wore silver-rimmed spectacles… and a black bowler hat. His rolled-up sleeves exposed a strange light beneath his skin. Half-turned away from the camera, his expression seemed one of startled surprise, as if the photographer had caught him unawares. The caption below the photograph read: *Shorepoint Depot, Turn of the Century (approx.).*

"I don't like that face, Thomas," Jeni whispered, shaking her head. "I don't like that face at all. There's something terrible about it." Jeni was right. In the crowd of sailors, the man stood out like a rotten weed. For a second it seemed as if the man's expression in the photograph changed as he gazed at it—his lips seemed to twist up into a wicked grin, as if he somehow felt Thomas's eyes upon him at that very moment! *Impossible!* Thomas thought, blinking rapidly. He could hear whispers gathering in the back of his brain that grew louder, building into a feverish chorus within his head, like the buzzing of approaching bees, until a cheerful voice silenced them.

"There you bookworms are!"

Thomas rubbed his eyes in disbelief. The man's expression was again surprised, his lips unmoving. Ms. Katz suddenly materialized behind them, as if coming up through a trap in the library floor. Her two hairless greyhounds, Bacchus and Bridget, trotted at her side, their nails clicking against the polished tile floor.

"What a fun project that was!" Ms. Katz cried, pushing her tortoise-shell glasses back up onto the bridge of her nose from where they were always slipping. Ms. Katz always favored bright colors in her wardrobe—bold purples and electric greens. Today she sported a mauve sweater that bubbled over her black leggings like a giant purple jellyfish.

"Mr. Tolbert," Ms. Katz continued, "who used to work here, as you will recall, wrote a local history of the dockyards before he passed away—what goods came in, what went out, the names of the ships, that sort of thing. Something tells me you bookworms might want to sink your teeth into that apple, hmmm?" Thomas and Jeni nodded.

(Just in case you weren't aware, bookworms don't have teeth, just strong mouth muscles that allow them to feed on microscopic molds and other organic matter.)

"Okay then!" Ms. Katz exclaimed enthusiastically. "Right this way!"

They followed Ms. Katz and her greyhound shadows to the library checkout desk where the librarian disappeared for a few moments behind a giant computer that must have been hi-tech twenty years ago but now took up half the desk. After a barrage of keystrokes, she let out a resounding, "Hot pickles!"—her own special expression, one Thomas and Jeni had heard at least twenty times a day when they had worked at the library. *Everything is checked back in and on the shelf, Ms. Katz,* they would say, to which the common reply was almost always, *Hot pickles!* as in *Holy spicy, vinegar-laden cucumber corpses!* (Yes, Ms. Katz was an odd duck.)

"Sorry to deflate your hopes, gang," said Ms. Katz, frowning. "But it seems Mr. Tolbert's book is already checked out."

"Checked out?" asked Jeni. "By whom?"

"Hmmm," said Ms. Katz. "It says here it was checked out by someone named Patrick Mulvaney. Do I know a Patrick Mulvaney?"

Patrick was Pop's real name! thought Thomas. *What would he want with a book about Gloomsbury's docks?*

"Thank you, Ms. Katz," he said, flashing Jeni a sideways glance.

"Not to be a meddling muskrat," said Ms. Katz, "but why are you two so interested in Mr. Tolbert's research? Not that I don't expect extracurricular probing from my two brightest pages."

When Thomas hesitated, Jeni stepped in.

"I'm doing a summer history project," she said, "for extra credit. I always wanted to know more about the docks. My grandfather used to work at Sneed Cannery, you know."

"Well, if that's the case," Ms. Katz said, snapping her fingers. "I may have just the thing! Bookworms, follow me!

Ms. Katz led them behind the library checkout desk and down a narrow corridor, Bacchus and Bridget clicking behind them at every step. The corridor snaked past mountains of water-spotted boxes stacked floor to ceiling—salvaged material from the great flood that had nearly washed the library away years ago. Ms. Katz pushed back a door and motioned Thomas and Jeni inside.

In the center of the room, a giant desk was covered with papers and half-finished tags to mark new releases, teen favorites, and Ms. K's Knockouts, her personal picks for that month's reading. Beside the desk, on a side table, a ceramic water steamer bubbled with hot water.

"Tea, anyone?" Ms. Katz asked.

"No, thank you," said Thomas and Jeni in rapid unison. They had sampled Ms. Katz's private blend of Nepalese tongue-root tea before, and both agreed it tasted about as good as it sounded.

"Suit yourselves," said Ms. Katz, pouring herself a cup of tea in a mug with the words *Reading is My Second Addiction* stenciled on its side.

Ms. Katz brushed some papers off two chairs and invited Thomas and Jeni to sit down.

"I wanted to show you something from Mr. Tolbert's files," she said. "But before I show it to you I have to ask. What is this really about? It can't be a school project, since school's out for summer."

"Thomas..." Jeni began. She bit her lip. "Fine! You might as well know because you might be able to help us. We think that Pop Mulvaney was murdered. I know it sounds crazy. But we've seen some people hanging around town we've never seen before. Strange people in dark suits and hats. Thomas saw them outside his house after Pop Mulvaney's body was dropped off at the funeral home. We don't think it's a coincidence."

"And I think I recognized one of the men I saw outside my house," said Thomas. "He's in that picture from the display. But it's impossible." He shook his head. "The date says that photo was taken over a hundred years ago."

"Let's say you two are on to something," said Ms. Katz. "Shouldn't you let someone know? Other than a librarian, I mean. The responsible authorities? The police?"

"That's the problem," said Thomas. "We don't have any real evidence yet. And there's nothing on Pop Mulvaney's body that suggests he was murdered. Jeni and I...we just feel like...like something's off."

"And you're good to trust that feeling, Thomas!" said Ms.

Katz waving her long pointer finger in the air like wand. "You know we share a distinct connection with animals. Sure, we drive cars, pay taxes, and all that hoopla, but our instincts are ancient—*primordial.* Just promise me you two will go to the police if things get sticky? Promise?"

"Yes," said Thomas.

"We promise," said Jeni nodding her head.

"Hot pickles!" Ms. Katz exclaimed, bring her hands together. "Now, fellow bookworms, feast your digestive juices on this!" She retrieved a black-and-white photograph from her desk drawer and handed it to Thomas and Jeni.

"It's the same photo as the one in the display," said Jeni, examining the photograph. "Wait…something's missing."

Thomas leaned in. Jeni was right. Everything was in its place: the man mending the fish net; the other man gutting fish; the shadow of the figure behind the mainsail. *But where was the man in the bowler hat next to the barrels?*

"I never mentioned it to anyone," said Ms. Katz, taking a long sip from her tea. "I thought maybe it was a mistake. Before all this digital photography, people had to develop photographs in darkrooms, which was a very painstaking process. Just the wrong bit of light or wrong balance of chemical can throw the whole shebang off. When you two showed up all interested in a project that *nobody* is interested in, I thought it high time to share that little discrepancy with you. The fact that Thomas says he believes he's seen this man before…How is that even possible? I don't know. But you're both right, something definitely feels off."

"Thank you, Ms. K." said Jeni. She handed the photo back to the librarian. "We better get going—"

"No, no, you bookworms hang on to it," said Ms. Katz. "You never know. Maybe it will come in handy."

"Okay," said Jeni. "Thanks, Ms. K."

Thomas's eyes wandered to the window. Through the mist and rain he could see a giant figure, his back to the window, raking leaves in the front yard of the library. The figure suddenly turned, as if sensing Thomas's gaze upon him. Thomas cringed. Two dark eyes set deep within a swarthy face stared back at him. A bushy moustache bristled over an unsmiling mouth. The man stared back at Thomas for a moment before Thomas, acutely uncomfortable, turned away.

"Oh, him?" said Ms. Katz, smiling. "Nothing gets by you, Thomas Creeper! I'm sure you all know Mr. Contenescu who works as sludge master for old man Sneed. He fixed that whole disaster with Gloomsbury Middle School's pipes last year, you may recall. That fossil of a fruitcake Sneed cut back Mr. Contenescu's hours, and he asked if he could do a little part-time work around the library." Ms. Katz stared around the disheveled office. A family of gerbils living in a shoebox made a tidier home. "Zeus knows we need the help," she said, smiling.

"Well, thanks again, Ms. Katz," said Jeni, rising to her feet. They left Ms. Katz to her work and her disgusting tea and navigated their way back through the byzantine corridor of stacked crates and file folders. Stepping out into the rain, Thomas tried to ignore the watchful gaze of the old Romanian, but he could feel his shifty black eyes boring into his skull. *What was his problem? Did he hate Creepers now, too, after working for the Sneeds all these years?*

"So Pop was a step ahead of us, huh?" said Jeni, scampering down the front steps of the library. "That's the Patrick Mulvaney who checked out the book, right?"

"Yeah," said Thomas in a distracted voice. Silvie had said something about a man disappearing on the beach, and the photo Ms. Katz showed them had demonstrated a man doing exactly that—in one picture and gone the next. *As if the photographer had caught him right before he disappeared into thin air.* And if this man could do that—*disappear and reappear whenever he wanted to*—wouldn't that mean he could do horrible things without ever getting caught?

"You know what we have to do, don't you?" Jeni said, coming to a sudden halt.

"Don't say what I think you're gonna say," said Thomas.

"You know it's the only way," said Jeni, tugging Thomas's arm. "If these guys are looking for something, something in Mr. Tolbert's book, something *Pop* found out about, then Pop probably stashed the book somewhere. Those creepy men on your street talked about a priest having something in his possession, right? Hey, are you even listening to me, professor?"

Thomas clamped his eyes shut and shook his head. *Why was Jeni Myers always right?* "This is crazy," he whispered. "We are *not* breaking into Pop Mulvaney's house."

But he didn't need to open his eyes to see that Jeni's mind was already made up. For when it was made up, there was nothing anyone, dead or alive, could do about it.

Elijah Creeper I

IV

Forensic Science, A Detective's Best Weapon

At the corner where their two neighborhoods diverged, Thomas and Jeni made their plan, although Thomas liked it about as much as a root canal.

They would sneak into Pop's cottage after his funeral (which was scheduled for the following morning). Jeni would tell her parents she wanted to help Thomas clean up after the service, and Thomas would tell his father he wanted to walk home. Uncle Jed would be riding with Thomas's father in the passenger seat of the old hearse so there wouldn't be space for Thomas in the Customline anyway, unless he wanted to ride in the back cabin where the caskets got stowed, which he surely did not. That would give them at least half an hour to break into the house, gather whatever evidence they needed, and get out. Since Pop's cottage was situated right on the grounds of St. Mary's, it would be easy to get from the gravesite to the cottage and get home before anyone was the wiser. At least that was their theory.

"I don't know what's in that house," said Jeni. "But I have a feeling we're not the only ones interested in something Pop knew or hid."

Suddenly, totally off-course from any playbook or plan, Jeni leaned in and gave Thomas a kiss on the cheek.

Thomas was stunned.

"Jen…I…"

"Don't get any grand ideas, professor," said Jeni. "It's just for luck. See you tomorrow at the funeral. *God…See you tomorrow at the funeral.* Doesn't that sound horrible?"

Jeni shuddered in a dramatic way, grinned, and then took off into the misting rain.

Thomas stood for a few moments, hand on his cheek, feeling as if a wasp had just flown up and stung him. He had never been kissed by a girl other than his own mother. It was a weird feeling, like being excited and wanting to vomit all at the same time. *Did he have feelings for Jeni Myers? Did she have feelings for him?* He couldn't imagine someone as smart and as pretty as Jeni liking someone as awkward and as miserable as him. There was just no way. Breathing normal air on the surface of Mars without your head exploding, he deduced, was a more likely scenario.

Thomas headed down Thayer, waving to Mrs. Gardner out of habit as he passed by her fence. The old widow stood in the rain, her hair net covering her curlers, holding her mail without any intention of getting out of the rain or of closing the mailbox lid. Thomas could still remember preparing her husband Gil's body for his funeral. One of the Gardners' relatives had chipped in to buy one of the more expensive caskets from Creeper & Sons—a Thermolux Repositor—and Mr. Creeper wanted to make sure everything was clean and polished. Thomas happened to be eating Skittles that day. At some point, during the casket polishing, a few Skittles slipped out of his hands and rolled under the velvet padding. The fabric was sewn tight and there was no easy way to get the candies out. He still thought about it from time to time. Somewhere *in* Gloomsbury Cemetery, Gil Gardner had Skittles under his legs.

Yanking open the front-porch door, Thomas could immediately sense something was wrong. The house was utterly silent. Thomas gasped. *He'd left his library books on the floor next to Ms. Katz's desk!* He had no proof of his visit to the library, no way of backing up his lie that he wanted to get a jump-start on his studies. And it was worse:

He was late.

The grandfather clock in the hallway struck five loud

clangs. On the last clang Mr. Creeper emerged from the Preparing Room.

"I…I'm sorry," Thomas stammered. "I lost track of time and—"

"Get out of my sight!" Mr. Creeper hissed as he stalked down the hallway toward Thomas, his face flushed bright crimson. "You wretched…lying…excuse for a…GET OUT!"

Thomas flew up the staircase and into his room, slamming the door behind him. He could hear his parents downstairs—the bird-like warble of his mother trying to calm his father down, followed by an angry tirade from his father. *Lying excuse for a son…*Those were the words his father had wanted to say. *His father wished it had been him, not David, who had died…*He wouldn't come out and say it in the open, but Thomas knew he was thinking it.

Thomas threw himself onto his bed and pulled a pillow over his head. But he couldn't block out the sounds coming from the first floor. *I hate my life. I hate my life*, he thought, over and over. *I wish I had been born into any other family in the world.* He couldn't even explain to his father that they were all in danger, that murderous things with glowing arms were watching their house—watching *them.* Nobody would listen to him even if he told them the house was on fire. He was a liar, a wretched excuse for a son. Those were his father's words. There was nothing left to say.

An hour later a knock sounded at the door.

From under his pillow, Thomas heard the door lock turn and unlock. It was his mother, he knew. She always came in after he and his father fought. Thomas heard the clatter of a plate on his desk, and a stench like over-roasted socks wafted through the room.

"I brought you some mushroom casserole, darling," his mother said, sitting down on the edge of his bed, but because she was so frail, the bed barely registered any shift in weight. She hesitated, then continued.

"Thomas…" she began. By the tone of her voice, Thomas

knew exactly what she was going to say. *He doesn't mean those things, darling...he just wants you to take your studies more seriously... do you think you could try a little harder? He has so much on his mind these days with the business.* Thomas tuned out his mother the best he could. *What right does she have in lecturing me?* he thought. *She doesn't care about what happened to me, only that I don't upset HIM.*

Thomas's mother patted his arm and left the room, the door closing quietly behind her. Thomas rolled over on his back and looked up at the ceiling. A sudden chill came over him. He glanced toward the window, but it was closed. He turned his head slowly and there she was.

Perhaps it was his promise to help her find her arm that gave Silvie Creeper a brighter glow. No longer afraid of her, Thomas found he could see her more clearly than ever before. She had the distinctly pale, pinched face of a Creeper, with dark eyes and a sharp chin. Her arm (the non-severed one) and legs, like his own, were spindly and thin. Her dress was strange and old-fashioned, and her dark hair was twisted into an ornate braid atop her head, just like in the old photographs from a half-century ago.

"I bet you're going to tell me I should be lucky I still have a mother," he griped.

Don't be a jerk! Silvie's voice echoed through his head. *Can you imagine losing a son?*

Thomas bolted up in the bed. "Losing a son? What about the son she still has?"

That's different.

"Yeah. It *is* different."

You need to check the priest's body, dumb-dumb. There's a clue on it. I'm sure of it. By tomorrow it'll be too late.

"A clue?" Thomas sighed. "My dad already hates me, and you think I should go…go poking around downstairs so he can have another reason to want to disown me?"

I said I would help protect you, didn't I? There has to be something on the priest that those guys are worried about someone finding. You really think he died of a heart attack? You think David died of a heart attack?

"Shut up!" said Thomas, stabbing a finger at the ghost-girl's face. "You have no right to talk about David! Go ruin some other person's life! I don't need your help!"

You do too, jerk! Maybe your dad is right. Maybe you are just a lying excuse for a son. Go check the priest's body, Thomas. You can apologize to me later.

"Apologize?" Thomas rolled his eyes. Now he was furious. "Why the hell would I—"

But she was gone.

Thomas groaned and pushed himself out of bed. The gray stew-like concoction steamed on a plate next to his bed, a new creation from Adele Creeper's demented cookbook. He picked up his fork and managed a few bites before spitting it into the trash can. *How did she manage to get a shellfish flavor in an asparagus and mushroom casserole?*

Silvie was right, Thomas knew. He had to check out Pop's body if he really wanted to know what was going on. He would have to wait until well after his father had gone to bed. And hope that nobody else in Gloomsbury died that night, bringing relatives of the deceased to the door and Elijah Creeper the Fifth out of his bed.

Thomas sighed and took the iPhone out of his desk drawer and powered it on. Maybe Jeni's cipher would take his mind off everything.

Thomas grabbed a notepad and pencil. He had learned from his reading that when people talked about breaking codes, they really meant ciphers. Ciphers were different from codes.

Ciphers masked words in gibberish by shifting letters around in a certain way chosen by the cipher's creator. The shifting was called *rotation.* For example, if you wanted to mask the word "dog" in cipher, you could rotate it one letter forward to make "eph." That was called a ROT1. Codes were different. They were like decoy substitutions for other words and phrases that you could understand only if you possessed the codebook. For example, a ship captain might tap out "the sea is stormy today" in Morse code, and someone with the codebook on the other end would understand it to mean "no enemy submarines sighted," or "Moby Dick is taking a personal day."

Jeni's cipher was pretty clever, but Thomas quickly noticed a pattern. It was a variation on a ROT1. When he rewrote everything using Jeni's ROT1 modification—she had shifted and then written the shift backwards—he stared back at the page full of scribbles. *No*, he thought. *It had to be wrong*…He went back and double-checked his work, then triple-checked it. But everything was right.

There it was, in the middle of the page, as clear as a Gloomsbury sun sighting:

Do you like me, Thomas Creeper?

That was what the "So?" e-mail with a hundred question marks was all about. He felt sick, but not from his mother's cooking. *Jeni Myers liked him*…and she wanted to know if he liked her back. The kiss on the cheek wasn't just for good luck. It was her way of saying she liked him.

He crumpled up the paper and stuffed it into his desk drawer. He slammed the drawer shut, as if he might seal the message inside forever like a tomb. He felt exhilarated and angry at the same time—exhilarated that someone could feel that way about him, and angry that things were changing between them. *What if they couldn't just be friends anymore?*

He crawled into bed and stared up at the ceiling in the darkness. *What right did she have?*

And then a strange thought like an annoying fly flitted across his mind:

What right did he have to say no if he felt the same way?

❧

He should have dreamt about something happy that night,

like discovering he could fly mid-dream, or that he had created an amazing kelp-and-seaweed sludge launcher to tangle up all the Gary Korvins of the world. But he didn't. Instead, he dreamt he was already at St. Mary's, only Pop Mulvaney wasn't dead, but still alive and leading the sermon.

Thomas was seated in the back row where he always sat, next to his mother and father under the stained-glass window of St. Michael gripping a large fiery sword. But in the dream the window was open. A curling fog swooped in through the window, and as it passed over Thomas's head the fog took shape, forming a long writhing arm with gently coaxing fingers. Jeni was seated a few rows ahead, her back to him. As if sensing Thomas's fear, the arm of fog stretched out over the pews until it hovered right over Jeni's head. Before Thomas could try to get Jeni's attention, the freezing hand pivoted rapidly, grabbing his wrist.

"You can't let them touch you, Thomas!"

It was David. His eyes were sunken and ringed by dark circles and his lips were blue and flecked with frost. His shirt hung about his frail body in tatters, and Thomas could see wormlike creatures squirming beneath his gray skin. A grating metallic screech suddenly filled the room, as if someone were slowly sawing a tin can in half. Thomas froze, fixed to the pew, as the grating grew louder and louder, though no one else seemed to notice.

"If they touch you, it's all over!" David rasped. "Look!"

Thomas turned. A man had risen to his feet in the front row and was staring at him—the same man in the bowler hat from the photograph at the library! His sleeves were rolled up to his elbows, and the markings on his arms swirled and pulsed with an eerie light. He waved at Thomas, then turned toward the pulpit. *But Pop Mulvaney didn't see him!* His back was turned away at the altar. Thomas had to warn him.

He turned to his parents for help. But his father just held a finger to his lips and told him to be quiet and "to show some respect here of all places." The man was just a few steps behind Pop now. The grating sound in the room reached a fever pitch. Pop turned, his eyes widening in horror. The man with the glowing arms reached out and placed his hand on Pop's chest, the wild light from his tattoos exploding like a solar flare. The room burst with blinding light as Pop let out a piercing scream.

Thomas awoke in the dark bedroom, the horrible scream lingering in his ears like the echo of a gunshot.

As his nerves settled and his breathing calmed, he thought of Jeni. He knew what she would say. She'd tell him that there were no coincidences, not even in dreams. The language of a dream might be harder to read—like Sanskrit instead of pigeon English—but there was a *reason* why he had seen the things he had. There was a reason David had warned him.

It wasn't until he was halfway down the staircase that he realized what he was doing. He and his father had gone over Pop Mulvaney's body meticulously and seen no evidence of foul play. *Still*…Silvie knew there was something on the body. *Maybe a ghost could see things the living had overlooked. Maybe*…

He knew where his father kept the key to the Preparing Room. It was hidden in the top right drawer of his study desk, inside a small metal tin that held the Carol brand razor blades he used for shaving. Thomas tiptoed through the foyer, avoiding the floorboards he knew from years of experience to be the loud talkers. He turned the study doorknob slowly, applying the slightest pressure here and there to control its desire to squeal and give him away. Keeping his head low, avoiding the stern gaze of The Elijahs, he made it around one side of the large black desk. From the drawer he fished out the key and a small flashlight. As he made his way back to the door his shoulders stiffened.

He could hear the books on the bookshelf moving in and out of place as if invisible hands gripped them. It had happened once before, when he tried to steal ten dollars from his father's petty cash drawer. He swore at the time that it was just his imagination working overtime, but when he looked at the shelf, he could see the books moving slowly in and out of place. The Elijahs were making their protest known.

Drawing up his brows, tonight he cast his worst, most fearsome stink-eye at The Elijahs, which probably only registered halfway on a normal person's scale. The books stopped their jostling. If it was his destiny to be the master of such a terrible house someday, he thought, then it was high time the house knew that the same cold blood of the Creeper Dynasty flowed through *his* veins, too. *Keep it up!* he told The Elijahs with his mind. *I'll turn Creeper & Sons into a sweet shop or a movie theater! Just try me!*

He fit the key into the Preparing Room door and turned the lock. Instantly the chill of the grave wafted over him. He clicked on the flashlight and played the small beam of light across the room to the cooler. He unlatched the cooler door, holding the flashlight between his teeth. Carefully, he pulled Pop Mulvaney out onto the cooling board. He pulled back the sheet and focused the flashlight's beam down on the body.

The old priest didn't look like a corpse anymore. Thomas's father had dressed him in the clothes Pop's family had sent—his old chaplain's uniform from his time in the Korean War. He had his usual white collar, but a small band of medals and distinctions were pinned over his left breast. His father had applied cosmetic touches around the cheeks and eyes to project a sense of good health. Thomas gritted his teeth and tried to focus. *There was a clue somewhere*...His father had missed it, he had missed it. But there was a clue there all the same.

Thomas undid Pop's jacket and shirt, cradling the flashlight between the crook of his neck and shoulder. He thought again of David's warning from the nightmare. But there was no mark on Pop's chest, no impressions left by a burning hand. It had just been a crazy dream, Thomas concluded, something he had conjured up while missing David and trying to make sense of something that was senseless.

He buttoned up the priest's shirt and jacket and pulled the sheet back over him. But he didn't close the cooling board. Not yet. His fingers gripped the sides of the freezing metal board until his knuckles turned white. He gritted his teeth. *There were no coincidences. There were no coincidences*, he repeated, closing his eyes. For a while in that second darkness behind his eyelids he didn't see anything, he just stood with the blood pounding in his ears, his breath rising and falling in the darkness. Then, like something floating up little by little from the bottom of a dark lake, he saw:

THE ENDLESS LIBRARY

It was an endless library of books, like a sunken city rising toward him.

He knew his photographic superpower worked only if he cared about something he had read. Anything about funeral life wouldn't make it onto the secret shelves of his hidden library. *But spies*...books about heists and the great code crackers of history, like the Polish team of cryptologists who had cracked the German Enigma Machine in 1932, those things stayed in his brain when everything else just faded away like tracks in the desert after a sandstorm.

Tonight the image of the hidden library in his mind came clearer than before. *Had Silvie done something to him when she gave him the Bond?* His eyes clenched tight; he thought about her words for a few seconds, and the image of the sunken library and its endless stacks wavered in and out. He took a deep breath and focused. The image crystallized again. He combed through the library in his mind until he found the spy book, his lips fluttering like a gypsy's trance. *C'mon! Show me! Show me what I'm supposed to do....*

A single page floated by, hovering clear and bright before his mind's eye:

Forensic Science. A detective's best weapon!

His eyes flashed open. *What did he know about forensics?* For starters, he knew it was the science of studying a crime scene.

A forensic scientist gathered data from a crime scene in order to form a rational understanding of what had happened. *Fingerprints!* His eyes lit up. What if there were fingerprints all over Pop Mulvaney's body; surely that would prove there had been some sort of foul play. But hours had passed since the old man had been brought in. How could he be sure there were any fingerprints left?

His heart sank. He felt as if he had pushed away confusion and doubt, only to find that truth had receded still further into an enigmatic gloom. He went back in his mind to the chapter on forensics in the spy book. *Argon lasers can detect fingerprints after a long period of time has elapsed...*but there was no way he was going to be able to find an argon laser, let alone get Pop Mulvaney's body under it before the morning. *But there was another way....*

Thomas remembered reading about it, though the words were fuzzy, hovering at the far margins of his mind. *Fingers left a residue of oil on whatever they touched.* But there was a way to make the oils reappear. He bit his lip until he drew blood. But he didn't care. He was right there. He could see it. *What was the secret? Tell me!* His fingernails dug into the palm of his hand. *Tell me! Don't leave me here so close with nothing to show for it!*

Out of the darkness behind his mind another page floated up like a rising moth:

IODINE

If Thomas could let out a *Eureka!* or *Hot Pickles!* he would have then. Under the right conditions, iodine fumes could make the residual oil left by fingerprints reappear! And because Thomas knew the Preparing Room like the back of his hand, having inventoried and re-inventoried every square inch for months, he knew that his father kept a small bottle of iodine tablets under the sink in an emergency crash kit, just in case the pipes in the old house went bad and they had to make drinkable water.

He found the bottle under the sink, right where it was

supposed to be from his inventory. *Okay*, he thought. *Now to turn the tablets into gas!* He retrieved a glass beaker from the cupboard and a lighter from the drawer. He poured hot water into the beaker, dropped the tablet inside, then flicked on the lighter and held it beneath the beaker. It was a long shot, but it had to work, he told himself. He put the flashlight on the cooling table and steadied it so it wouldn't roll off. He waited for what seemed like an eternity. And then the beaker started to smoke.

He unbuttoned the priest's shirt and jacket, hoping the smoke alarm at the far end of the room wouldn't go off. But he didn't care. He had to know the truth. *Don't let them touch you!* David had warned in the dream. He could hear his father's caustic voice. *What is the source of all life, Thomas, the wellspring of aortic pressure and fluid that controls all thought and action?* He held the beaker under the beam of light, wafting the fumes frantically toward the old man's bare chest. *The heart. The heart is life*, he thought. *The heart is everything.*

But nothing happened. No mark appeared, no residue left from the oils of fingerprints.

Crestfallen, he slumped back against the side of a metal trolley that held his father's embalming tools. He felt like smashing the beaker against the wall. And he would have if suddenly, there in the white light of the flashlight's beam, five distinct brown-colored splotches hadn't appeared over the old man's chest.

There were no other marks, no outline of the hand itself. If these were Pop Mulvaney's prints and he had clutched his own chest in pain, then part of the hand would have shown up. But no—*here were the tips of five fingers, like five red-hot pokers pressing down over Pop Mulvaney's heart....*

Tears filled Thomas's eyes. *He wasn't crazy!* Even as the five brown marks started to disappear, the chill of the room swallowing the last of the iodine fumes, he finally had evidence, proof of foul play. Pop Mulvaney had been murdered, and maybe his brother David, too, and those who had done the horrible deeds were still out there in Gloomsbury and had been for years. They were the town's oldest, darkest secret.

And it was up to him to make sure they never killed again.

BOOK TWO:
Sinkholes, Sinking Feelings,
and Two Sinking Ships

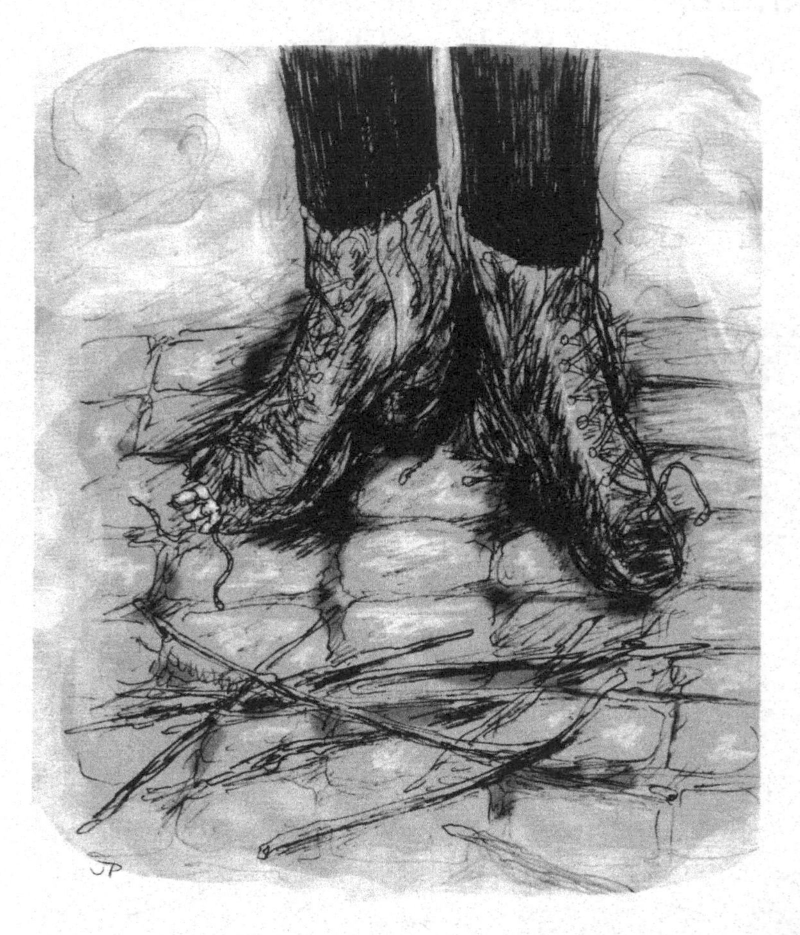

V

"Hello, boy!"

The next morning, the day of Pop Mulvaney's funeral, Thomas awoke with a frenzied sense of urgency.

He showered, dressed in his usual funeral attire—an ancient black suit with a matching black vest that had once belonged to his great uncle Ernest, back when people stuffed their clothes with mothballs. He took a whiff of the vest and nearly gagged. At least the smell might keep Jeni from trying to kiss him again.

Whirling down the staircase, he arrived just in time to see his father and Uncle Jed at the door to the Preparing Room door, arguing over how best to transfer Pop's body from the cooling board to the casket trolley.

"How many times do I need to tell you, Jedidiah?" snarled Elijah Creeper the Fifth. "You must grip from *under* the arms, not around the waist! *Under* the arms! You want him floundering like a…like a *fish* stuck on a line?"

"And how many times have I told *you*, brother o' mine," Jed snapped back. "You're gonna scrape the old man's ass! Oh, hullo, Tommy Boy!"

The two faces—the two very different faces of Elijah Creeper the Fifth and Jedediah Creeper—stared up at Thomas.

"You know your duties?" his father barked impatiently.

"Yes," said Thomas. He was supposed to clear the path of any sticks so that the pallbearers wouldn't trip carrying the casket to the gravesite. He had done it a million times before, and yet his father still insisted on asking him if he knew how to do a task a monkey could probably do blindfolded.

"Good," said Thomas's father. "I'll see you at the service. No dilly-dallying." Thomas watched his father and Jed place Pop's body down onto an ancient contraption—the casket trolley—a many-wheeled wooden creation of their father's, Elijah Creeper the Fourth, that still bore the dents and nicks of his dangerous riding crop. How the two brothers had managed to not kill each other all these years seemed a sheer miracle to Thomas.

Thomas stepped out onto the porch and patted his jacket pockets, checking his supplies. He had his flashlight and his trusty penknife, a gift from his uncle Percival, who lived in an old lighthouse in Nova Scotia where he wrote fiction reviews for the *New Yorker* and the *Guardian*. The phrase "a writer is never alone when he has words" had been inscribed on the blade. Thomas secretly dreamed that one day, when his father finally gave up trying to turn him into a mortician, he would go live with Uncle Percival and learn about how a writer takes ideas and feelings and crafts them into stories. That certainly seemed like a better life than the one his parents had chosen for him. There would be less blood at least. The penknife wouldn't do much good against beings that could appear and disappear at will and kill with a touch, but it made him feel better just the same.

The service for Pop Mulvaney was short but heartfelt. After reading a few items from scripture, a man with a hawkish face and a thousand laugh lines around his mouth said a few words about his "old friend and comrade Patrick Mulvaney, a real genuine article if ever there was one." He told the congregation about their great friendship through four decades: how Pop had helped him and his wife find a new home, mentored their two children, and even assisted with the installation of an underground sprinkler system in their garden. Thomas's eyes lit up upon hearing this anecdote. Pop Mulvaney had been a man of many talents, though few had known it. From across the hushed room he caught sight of Jeni. She caught his gaze and winked at him, and he quickly looked away, heat flooding his cheeks.

After a few other speakers said their eulogies, the choir sang a recessional. Thomas hastily wiped a few tears from his cheeks before anyone could notice. He swallowed several times, trying to rid himself of the lump in his throat. He was going to miss Pop.

Since he was seated near the back of the church, it wasn't hard to sneak out before the recessional ended. One of the ushers, Tad Covington, smiled and nodded to him as he had smiled and nodded a hundred times before and opened the large oak doors to let him out. Thomas made his way between the tall hedges, climbing the wet, moss-covered stone steps toward the cemetery. He could see the Customline already parked up ahead, its muffler rattling next to a giant stone monument to one of the Sneed family. There weren't many sticks to collect that morning. The undertaker, Morris Wells, was old, but not too old to take care of his daily tasks around the cemetery, and he kept the grounds fairly clean. Head down, picking up sticks, Thomas didn't notice he had wandered off the main path.

He had unknowingly crossed into the east side of the cemetery, a place he seldom went because the warped brass doors of the mausoleums reminded him of yawning mouths, and the dog-faced gargoyles and the weeping statues of angels gave him the chills. A wet fog started to draw up around his collar. It began close to the ground, then rose, swelling up and around the high obelisks and monuments to the Sneed family and the crumbling headstones that marked the resting places of their poor cousins, the Fipps. Soon the path at Thomas's feet was obscured by a sea of fog, as if dry ice had wafted up from cracks in the wet earth. A gust of wind struck up out of nowhere, clearing the mist and fog at his feet. As it all swirled away, he found himself staring down at a pair of cracked black leather shoes.

"Hello, boy," a voice rasped like dry leaves scuttling across pavement. Thomas lifted his head, promptly dropping the bundle of sticks at his feet. His whole body trembled. The face staring down at him seemed attached to its skull by the most unskilled of stitching. The skin hung in loose white folds around cheekbones that jutted out sharp and bare. Two glittering black eyes peered down at Thomas from beneath the shadowed brim of a rain-soaked bowler hat.

"You have taken such good care of the dead," the man whispered, coming closer. "And to be around death from such a tender age, well. . . ."

Run! Get the hell out of here! he thought. But he couldn't move. His legs felt as if they were anchored to the earth. His mouth felt parched as if he hadn't had a sip of water in days. The man reached out a sickly white hand. Fingers, the nails long and cracked and amber-yellow, hovered a few inches above Thomas's pounding heart. The fingers curled into a claw, as a light appeared in the dark, sunken eye sockets. Above the man's bare wrist the tattoos started to swirl and writhe, growing wilder and wilder, just as they had in Thomas's nightmare. *This is it*, thought Thomas, paralyzed with fear inside the field of light. *This is how it ends.*

As Thomas stood, rigid with fear, he became aware of voices on the wind. The congregation were leaving the church! He tried to call for help, but his voice was frozen in his throat. *You will give up this audacity, Thomas Creeper!* The man's raspy voice echoed in Thomas's head, just as Silvie's had done. *Follow your brother's path and you risk the same fate! And that fool Mulvaney—see how his meddling ended with the grave! Whoever challenges the Sieve shall know our vengeance!*

The light receded. The fingers at Thomas's chest moved up, toward the lapel of his jacket and righted the drooping boutonniere that had come loose from its pin.

"Farewell, Thomas Creeper," the man whispered, stooping to bend his long torso into a little bow. "You have been warned."

With that, the man removed a pair of small wire-rimmed glasses from his pocket, and placing them on the bridge of his rotting nose, disappeared completely. The cemetery swam in Thomas's peripheral vision, the ground and sky inverting. Then the world and everything in it went dark.

❧

Thomas awoke gasping for breath, the earth a damp chill against his cheek. The swirling fog was gone. He staggered to his feet, stumbled past the moss-covered headstones, and raced around to the rear of the church, where the congregation was now gathered around Pop's open grave.

Heart still pounding, Thomas found his place behind Jeni and her parents near the back row. His father, fortunately, seemed unaware of his son's brief absence, distracted as he was by the service.

It was time for the part of the ceremony Elijah Creeper the Fifth detested the most—the tossing of the dirt. Even modestly priced as Pop Mulvaney's casket was, to Thomas's father it seemed a cardinal sin to profane such excellent craftsmanship and dedication. Everyone made the rounds to pay their last respects to Pop Mulvaney, everyone except Elijah Creeper the Fifth.

As the funeral party started to thin out, Jeni turned to her parents to ask permission to help Thomas with his duties. Taking his cue, Thomas approached the Customline hearse, dusting off the remaining dirt and mud from his suit so his father wouldn't notice and launch into another lecture from Creeper Family Protocol. He found his father and Uncle Jed inside the hearse, embroiled in yet another argument. Jed was accusing Thomas's father of ignoring the fact that the car's clutch had long been in need of repair.

"Mind your forked tongue!" Elijah Creeper the Fifth bellowed from the front driver seat, stabbing a long finger in his brother's half-masked face. "You have no business counseling me in matters you've abandoned!"

"Abandoned?" Jed shot back. "If I didn't do your dirty work day in and day out…"

Thomas knew there would be no use trying to get a word in edgewise. He left the two brothers arguing in the idling car, the windows now rolled up completely so that the heated debate would not be overheard by any remaining passersby, thereby sullying the professional image of Creeper & Sons Funeral Services.

Thomas could see Jeni approaching from the wings. He strode toward her, but found himself waylaid by the braces-faced boy wonder, Arnold Myers.

"Look, Creeper, I know you hate my guts," said Arnold. "But Jen told me about something weird going on with Pop and I—"

Jeni looked over at Thomas and shot him a pleading look. She had been waylaid herself—by Mrs. Nowitzki who likely was asking Jeni to volunteer again for the church's summer bake sale.

"I guess what I'm trying to say is that you might not be such a pansy after all," Arnold continued. "Plus, Jen's my sister. I can't let you get her involved in all this stuff without the proper protection, you know? So check it out!"

After Arnold was certain no one was watching them, he opened the folds of his suit jacket. Thomas shook his head in amazement. All sorts of fireworks were taped to the lining of Arnold's jacket—long slender bottle rockets, round M-80s, and something that looked like a dragon with a long fuse coming out of its mouth.

"Face it, Creeper," said Arnold, flashing a cocky smile. "You need me. For firepower!"

"We don't need you *or* your firepower," said Thomas, as Jeni finally broke away from Mrs. Nowitzki.

"Oh, I think you do, Creeper," Arnold replied with a smug smirk as he buttoned up his arsenal.

"Arnold, give us a second, would you?" Jeni asked. When Arnold wouldn't budge, in pure Arnold Myers fashion, Jeni shouted a muffled, "GET LOST!" and gave Arnold a swift shove. Sulking and grumbling under his breath, Arnold retreated to a nearby willow tree, where he leaned against the trunk, arms folded over his bulky jacket.

"What did you tell him, Jeni?" said Thomas. "If we get into trouble that idiot's going to get us killed."

"He means well," said Jeni. "Face it, we could use the numbers. It's not like two against a mob of psycho killers is the best odds."

Thomas looked over at Arnold and grimaced. He was playing with a Zippo lighter, jerking the cover open and closed, smiling when he could get the flame to click on, which happened about one in every ten tries. "Fine," Thomas conceded. "But if he screws this up, it's your fault, not mine."

"Fine," said Jeni.

Thomas turned to go, but Jeni grabbed his arm.

"Hey! Did you crack my cipher yet?" she asked, her green eyes wide and flashing.

"Not yet," he mumbled. "Sorry."

"Are you okay, Thomas? You look kinda pale, paler than normal, that is," Jeni said.

"Yeah, but something awful happened. I'll tell you about it on the way to Pop's house." He paused. "Let's go before Arnold sets himself on fire and ruins everything."

They made their way west through the church grounds, on the path that led to the outbuildings and Pop's small cottage.

As they walked, Thomas told Jeni about the marks on Pop's chest, the evidence that proved he'd been murdered. Then he told her of his frightening encounter in the cemetery with the man in the black bowler hat, the paralyzing field of light, and the man's whispered warning. Jeni stopped short in horror.

"Thomas!" she cried, tears in her eyes. He had never seen Jeni get all mushy with tears or break down or anything, not even after she slammed her head into the goalpost and had to get stitches.

"Don't you ever do that again, Thomas Creeper!" Jeni wailed, punching him in the shoulder.

"Ow! What's that for? Don't ever do what?" Thomas yelled.

"Don't ever do anything that dangerous without me," Jeni growled.

A moment later, they crouched down by Pop's old station wagon and studied his stone cottage. The house had a small, well-manicured yard. Had it been any other day, they might have seen plumes of smoke from the chimney. Pop often sat before the fire, preparing sermons or reading Swedish mysteries about dark deeds in the snowbound reaches of the Land of the Midnight Sun. But there was no sun today in Gloomsbury, Land of Perpetual Gloom, no smoke curling out the chimney, only fog wafting over the hedges and around the shadows on either side of the cottage.

"So, we're breaking into his house?" Arnold said, rising to his feet as Jeni jerked him down by his suit jacket.

"How should we do it, Thomas? Smash a window?" asked Jeni.

"Alarm," Thomas and Jeni both said in unison, nodding at each other.

"We could knock the doorknob off," said Arnold. "I saw that on *C.S.I.* once."

"Knock it off with what?" scoffed Thomas.

They looked around the yard and spotted a coiled hose and an empty wheelbarrow, but no large rocks, nothing sharp with which they could bash in a doorknob. Thomas thought about wrapping his fist with his jacket and punching the glass panel in the door, but getting his palm sewn up by Elijah the Creeper the Fifth wasn't the way he wanted to spend his evening.

"C'mon, Thomas," said Jeni. "*Think*. You're good at this stuff. How do we get in?"

Thomas pressed his hands against his temples, furrowing his forehead in intense concentration. He tried to contact the secret library, sifting the stacks for something he'd read somewhere in a spy novel with garrote wire and zip-lines. But there was no tingle, no page fluttering up clear and bright in the darkness of his mind's eye. But then he realized he didn't need the library. A memory of a fun afternoon came flooding into his brain. *Pop at the window smiling. Voices in the yard. Shouts of play and...a crash of broken glass.*

"Hot pickles!" Thomas exclaimed.

"This is not the time for Ms. Katz impressions, Thomas—" Jeni began.

"C'mon!" Thomas said, grabbing Jeni by the wrist and jerking her up. Arnold followed a few steps behind.

When they got to the side of the house Thomas stopped. "Remember Volunteer Day?" he whispered to Jeni. "Tyler Neff kicked that soccer ball at Jake Shepherd and—"

"Jake moved out of the way!" said Jeni, finishing the thought. "The ball broke that storm window in the basement of Pop's house."

The fog swirling around the stone cottage parted, revealing a black trash bag blowing in the cellar window. It was just their luck: the old priest hadn't gotten around to fixing the window yet. Dropping to his knees before the opening, Thomas took out his penknife and cut a hole in the black bag. They all held their noses and gasped. The smell was worse than Arnold's breath. It smelled like mildew and decay had had a party and forgot to clean up.

"You sure Pop Mulvaney didn't die in there?" said Jeni, grimacing.

"Pretty sure," said Thomas, slipping feet-first into the dark cellar. "Dead bodies smell a whole lot worse than that."

❧

Once his feet touched solid ground, Thomas turned back to help Jeni clamber through the window. Today his lanky height was a gift. Arnold, on the other hand, refused to be "manhandled" and fought his way down the best he could...

which was the best he could. Fortunately, a pile of what felt like damp cardboard broke his fall.

"Don't suppose…Pop Mulvaney…kept any flashlights?" Jeni whispered, her hand covering her mouth. The smell was even stronger in the cellar than it had been outside and Thomas shivered, wondering if they had stumbled into some underground rat nest.

Arnold took a few steps and immediately banged into something metal that clattered to the ground.

"Nice work, Einstein," said Jeni. "We're not gonna be much help to Pop Mulvaney if we can't see—"

Feeling a beaded string brush against his cheek, Thomas reached up, wrapped his cold fingers around it, and yanked down hard. Soft light filled the cellar, illuminating stone walls stained with mold and trickling with humidity.

"Hot pickles!" Jeni gasped. "What in the world did you get yourself into, Pop Mulvaney?"

Thomas's eyes adjusted. Now he, too, could see what Jeni was gaping at.

Beyond the ghost-like forms of draped sheets covering boxes and furniture, he could see something hanging from a far wall above an old chandelier gathering rust on the floor.

It was a giant map.

It covered the cellar wall from floor to ceiling. The top of the map was pinned to the wall, its edges yellowed and curled. Furious notes covered the surface of the map like the scribblings of some mad scientist. But as Thomas inched closer, he could see that the lines formed buildings. It was a map of the whole town of Gloomsbury—every structure and street, every dock and seawall. Thomas squinted behind his glasses, their surfaces fogged with damp perspiration. Strange small circles dotting the map. He wiped the wet lenses of his glasses and peered closer.

The circles weren't circles at all.

They were human skulls with plus and minus signs next to them.

"Wh-what's with all the skulls?" whispered Arnold.

"I don't know," said Jeni shaking her head and drawing in a deep breath. "They can't be…I mean they can't all be murders, Thomas, can they? Look at this one." She planted her finger over a small skull with *+- 1897 Elijah Creeper* inscribed next to it. "What year did you say they found the note Elijah Creeper the First left?"

"1897," answered Thomas in a quiet, distracted voice. *What had Pop Mulvaney gotten himself into?* A dry, sour taste started to fill his mouth, the way he imagined a corpse might feel—if it could feel—with all those cotton balls shoved between its cheeks. His gaze followed the streets detailed in the map up from the marshes of Sarah's Lament to Town Beach, through the skull-dotted streets of Thayer Row and The Uppercrust to a square-shaped sketch of a house, a house with a gabled roof and turret.

It was his house, Thomas realized with horror.

The cypress trees were sketched in, as was the shingled roof…and the name. Thomas blinked his eyes a couple of times, wishing that the words would disappear. The name next to the skull on the map remained unchanged—David Creeper.

Thomas staggered backward. He felt sick. Jeni caught him in an awkward hug. She stared up into his eyes until he couldn't look at anything but her.

"It's all true, isn't it?" Jeni said in a voice choked with emotion. "No coincidences! Pop had been following them all along. He got too close and they killed him for it. If these skulls are right, the Sieve have been in Gloomsbury for centuries. Look! There's a skull with 1878 written next to it."

Suddenly, a breeze passed through the room, gusting in from the hole in the trash bag and causing the center part of the map to become momentarily concave…*as if something was behind it!* Thomas unpinned the corner of the map and pulled it aside to reveal a doorway without a door.

There was a hidden room behind the map.

"Holy crap!" Arnold shouted in excitement.

"Shhhh!" Jeni whispered. "Keep your voice down! We don't want anyone to know we're down here."

Thomas played the beam of his flashlight through the opening of the hidden door, then stepped forward into the room. Jeni followed close behind and Arnold after her, muttering something about black widow spiders.

The doorway opened into a small, dank room, whose central feature was a large desk upon which a half-melted candle sat enclosed within a dusty hurricane lantern. There were other items on the desk, each one covered in a thick film of dust: a box of matches, a few discarded and burnt—the long-stemmed kind his father used to light the candelabras in the house when the power went out. There were several books, one of them open and resting on top of the pile. Thomas moved the beam of the flashlight. A large crucifix hung on the wall above the desk, paint chips flaking off the face of Christ. Jeni took a match from the matchbox and struck it. The wick caught and warm yellow light filled the underground room, making it seem almost cozy. *Almost.*

Jeni raised a finger to her lip as she scanned every detail of the room, floor to ceiling, taking everything in like a trained detective. Dusty footprints could be seen on the cellar floor, but they were smudged by dirt and time, and Jeni couldn't tell if they'd belonged to one person or several.

"Well, there's the book from the library," she said, gesturing toward the desk where Mr. Tolbert's research project, *Gloomsbury: Then and Now*, lay open. "Look, it's open to that same photo with that creep," said Jeni, wiping dust from the page. "And there's a caption under it." She furrowed her brow and read fine type: *Crowley's Trollers. Gloomsbury Bay, 1888....*"

Jeni pulled another book from the stack and flipped through its pages.

"Thomas," she exclaimed excitedly. "I think...no, I'm right! It's Pop's diary!"

Thomas listened as Jeni read one of the earliest entries dated March 6th, 1946.

"Pop couldn't have been much older than you or me when he wrote this," said Jeni. "He says he followed a strange man, wearing a round hat and spectacles, who he'd seen leaving a house on Quarry Street." Jeni swallowed hard. "Right after Pop heard a woman scream." Jeni glanced up at Thomas, her eyes wide in the flickering candlelight.

"Listen to this," Jeni said, reading on. "Pop talks about seeing one of them for the first time, one of the Sieve. He says, 'When I caught up to him, the man turned slowly at the sound of my footsteps, grinning horribly. He reached out his hand and started coming toward me. But then, out of nowhere, a car hurtled into him, knocking him clean into the air. Somehow I had the instinct to jump back right as the car barreled past. When I recovered my wits, I found to my amazement that there was no body. The driver and I searched for some time but we found neither blood nor bone, nor indeed any evidence that the man had ever been there at all. Just a pair of wire-rimmed glasses, miraculously intact, lying beside the pavement.' What do you think that means, Thomas?" Jeni asked, glancing up again from the page.

"It's just like the man in the cemetery this afternoon," Thomas said in a shaky voice. "He put on a pair of glasses and disappeared—"

"Disappeared?" asked Arnold nervously, eying the dark corners of the cellar. "That's actually a great idea. Why don't we disappear, too? Seems like there's nothing—"

"Not so fast," said Jeni. "There has to be something else down here, something Pop hid that he didn't want anyone to find. Why else would you keep a secret room?"

Thomas moved towards the crucifix on the wall, wiping his foggy glasses on his shirt. *If Pop had something dangerous, something that might get him killed, where would he hide it?* he mused.

Pop was a man of faith, he thought. *A man who believed in a higher power that could counteract all evil.* At the base of the crucifix, he saw arc-shaped scratches along the wall. "Jeni, look at this!" he exclaimed.

"Wow!" she said, tracing the scratches with her finger. "What could have made scratches in stone like this?"

"It's almost as if the cross moves like…like a pendulum," Thomas muttered to himself. Pushing against the base of the crucifix, it slid across the wall like a hand on a clock.

"Holy crap," Arnold wheezed, shining the flashlight beam on the wall to reveal a small dark hole. Thomas reached into the hole and brought out a small object wrapped in a string of black rosary beads. Unwrapping the object, he found an old pair of wire-rimmed spectacles.

"What is it, Thomas? What did you find?" Jeni asked from behind him. "Are those glasses? I think Pop mentions something about glasses in his diary." Her voice sounded faint and muffled, as if it were coming to his ears from the far side of the moon. Slowly, he took off his own glasses and replaced them with the wire-rimmed spectacles.

"It's right here, Thomas. He says 'I have seen them throughout time using the glasses,'" read Jeni. "'It's a trick—no, a weapon, I think. I can see their true faces. But I can only wear the glasses for a short while or else they will see me. The fog falls away…and their faces start'…what does it say?" Jeni paused. "I can't make the writing out. 'The faces start to turn toward me and'…NO! THOMAS! STOP! WAIT!"

But it was too late.

The glasses settled onto Thomas's nose and the room and everything he saw in it disappeared.

VI

Combine or Die

For what seemed like forever, Thomas fell through a wormhole of mist, until he landed, sprawled, in chilly sand.

He pushed himself upright. It was near dark. Whether it was the faint twinkling of daybreak or dusk, he couldn't tell. Salt air filled his lungs. Fog hung in thick, curling swoops. Fingers of fog reached out for him, circling around his neck, wrapping around his wrists and ankles like manacles. He kicked out and the strange grasping fog retreated a little.

What happened to the cellar? Where were Jeni and Arnold? He remembered putting on the wire-rimmed spectacles, right before the world dematerialized and he began falling through the wormhole.

He was standing on the side of a steep bank of sand. Long stems of wild grass fluttered all around him. Down below the fog and gathering mist he could make out the dark shroud of the ocean. The moon was coming out. It was nighttime, he realized. The first silver streaks of moonlight painted the waves below. Over his shoulder, back through the fog, he could discern the sharp angles of houses, storefronts, a church. A church that looked exactly like St. Mary's by the Sea with its massive stained-glass window shaped like a sail and a stone cross at the top. *He wasn't on the far side of the world at all!* He was standing atop Dyre Dunes, the massive bluffs that overlooked Gloomsbury Bay.

Suddenly, he heard voices coming from the beach down below.

Clambering down one side of the dune, digging his hands into the beds of wild grass for support, he reached the level sand of the beach. In the moonlight he could see two men gathered around a boat bobbing in the low surf. One of the men waded through the surf, loading crates onto the back of the boat, while the other stood watch on the beach, his arms crossed over his chest.

Keeping his head down low, Thomas scrambled over to a giant rock covered with barnacles, about twenty feet from the shore, and hunkered down behind it. The men were locked in an argument. He strained his ears, hoping to hear what they were saying.

"You must bury it, Sneed!" one of the men shouted. "There's too many of them. If they recover it, we're all doomed!"

"I don't take orders from a Creeper!" Sneed snarled, turning back from the boat and stabbing his finger toward Creeper. "We're only working together on this because we have no choice! I don't answer to you…you or your infernal family!"

Creeper and Sneed working together? Thomas shook his head dumbstruck. *It wasn't possible! Who was he looking at?* He had to get closer.

He scurried over to the next rock until he was only ten feet or so from the two men. His heart pounded in his chest. Beads of sweat dotted the sides of his temples. He peered around the rock and watched as the men pushed the boat into the deeper surf.

Sneed climbed into the boat and grabbed the oars while Creeper stood in the knee-high surf, watching him go. The clouds shifted overhead. Moonlight lit up the shoreline like a great spotlight. Thomas gasped. *He knew that face!* It had glared down at him from the walls of his father's study ever since he could remember. Like the beam of moonlight, everything came into startling focus in Thomas's mind. *The glasses didn't allow you just to jump from place to place, but from* TIME *to* TIME!

His eyes widened as he beheld the bewildering but familiar visage—the fine moustache and oiled hair, the stooped shoulders that were the trademark of his funereal kinsmen. He was looking at Elijah Creeper the First!

There were a million things Thomas wanted to ask his ancestor. *What was the meaning of his last message, that enigmatic final word: WORMS?* Thomas crept closer, sand crunching under his feet, despite his best efforts to move like a secret spy. All was well until, reaching out to balance himself, he dislodged a rock, which toppled into a rock pool with a loud splash.

Thomas froze, wincing, at the sound, certain he had given himself away. But Elijah the First's expression remained unchanged. Thomas picked up another stone and threw it against the rock with a loud clatter, but Elijah Creeper the First didn't so much as move or turn his head. His theory was right. *The glasses made him invisible!*

Sneed was a skilled oarsman and was soon beyond the first ring of jetties into deeper water. As the boat disappeared into the fog, Elijah Creeper the First turned away and trudged through the surf back to the beach. Thomas crept closer, until he was right up next to his ancestor's shoulder, although his presence seemed no more discernible to Elijah Creeper the First than a ghost raising the hairs on the back of one's neck.

"All luck go with you, Sneed," Elijah Creeper the First whispered. "In this damned business I'm afraid we are partners. May the sea swallow you before they know what we've discovered!"

Suddenly, a weird sound—like a bird screeching, only louder than any bird Thomas had ever heard—pierced the salty air.

"Damn! The devil is quick!" said Elijah Creeper the First, straightening in shock and peering over Thomas's invisible head toward the bluffs. He reached into a pocket in his vest. With a shaking hand he withdrew a large silver flask. Emptying the contents of the silver flask around him in a circle he shouted, "You cannot cross the circle! The holy fire protects me!"

Thomas glanced up to see faces materializing above the dunes: dark, sinister eyes glittered wickedly beneath dark hats. A tall man led the pack, his arms glowing with shifting, swirling light.

Elijah Creeper the First lit a match. The tip broke off and fell into the sand. He cursed and lit another. The second match broke the same as the first. The figures crept closer. On the third try the flame sputtered and caught. Elijah the First threw the flaming match to the ground. The circle of liquid at his feet burst into sapphire-blue flames. Thomas leapt backwards, feeling a wall of heat ripple over him. In the light of the sapphire flames Thomas could see the figures' faces as they came closer: pale and sickly looking, each one grinning with stained yellow teeth. The words Jeni had spoken right before Thomas had put on the enchanted glasses echoed through his mind: *I can see them—their true faces. But something tells me to wear the glasses for only a short while or else they will see me.*

Elijah Creeper the First, now recognizing Thomas's presence somehow, shouted to him behind the wall of blue fire. But as his lips moved, the sound that came from his throat wasn't his voice.

It was Jeni's.

"Wake up! Wake up, Thomas Creeper! Or so help me God, I will make you eat those glasses!"

"Wait!" shouted Thomas as a hand—a small, pale hand with pink-painted nails —appeared in the sapphire light, fingers grasping around the frames of his wire-rimmed spectacles. "No! Wait! Tell me!" Thomas shouted to Elijah Creeper the First. "What's in the boat? Tell me! What did you find?"

Jeni's hand—for now he recognized it as hers—jerked the glasses off his nose. He felt himself whipped up in the gusts of a tornado as the world of the beach and the blue sapphire light retreated to a fine point beneath him.

When his eyes flashed open, Thomas found himself on the cold ground of the cellar, his chest rising and falling like a demented bellows. Jeni leaned over him, her face drawn up in a mask of terror, the wire-rimmed spectacles clutched in one hand. Over her shoulder he could see Arnold holding the lantern, his mouth open in startled shock.

"Thomas, I—" she began, with an angry scowl. For a second, Thomas thought she might punch him. And she probably would have if they hadn't been startled by a horrible sound coming from the floor above.

"I told you someone would hear us," Jeni said to Arnold. She helped Thomas back onto his feet.

"What?" said Arnold. "It wasn't me! He was the one screaming! Yell at *him*!"

"I was screaming?" said Thomas.

"Like a baby," said Jeni. She handed him back the enchanted glasses. "I wouldn't put those on again if I were you."

"Agreed," said Thomas. He placed the enchanted glasses back in his pocket and put on his ordinary, non-time-traveling glasses. "Now what do we do? Any ideas?" he whispered.

The cellar door cracked open and a dagger of light cut across the stairs. Thomas grabbed Jeni's wrist. "I'll get you out the window," he said. "You go get help—"

"I'm not going anywhere, Thomas Creeper," said Jeni, breaking the feeble wristlock. She was well trained in the feeble attempts of brothers and other boys to mess with her. "If it's the Sieve we're all dead anyway. Now grab something, you idiots—anything. I don't plan on dying in some dead priest's basement. You—Arnold! Do something useful for once in your life."

"DID YOU SAY USEFUL?" In the light of the single swaying light bulb, Arnold Myers stood like a madman. A fistful of fireworks were clenched tightly in his outstretched hands, the fuses already smoking.

"Arnold! No! I didn't mean that!" Jeni shouted. "Wait! You'll burn us all alive!"

But waiting wasn't a word in Arnold Myers's vocabulary. There were too many things to blow up, and waiting just got in the way. He leaned back.

"SAY 'ELLO TO MY LEEEEETLE FRIEN—"

The room exploded in a kaleidoscopic cacophony of light and sound. A thousand curling, corkscrewing pops of yellow, green, and red danced and zinged all around Thomas and Jeni as they huddled helplessly, hands covering their ears. Arnold had unleashed his "grand finale"—his favorite personal selections from Sparky's Online Firework Bonanza, outlawed in thirty-six U.S. states.

Amid all the cracking and popping they almost didn't hear the shrill voice crying out in terror from the cellar stairs. "Stop! Please stop! Don't kill me! I just want to talk!"

The last firework fizzled out. The cloud of noxious smoke and fumes parted. A figure stood at the bottom of the cellar stairs. His hands were held high in surrender, and there was a look of genuine terror on his face, a face Thomas Creeper immediately recognized.

❧

During the meeting in his father's study, Richie Mulvaney had made Thomas feel ill at ease, but today, after almost getting blown up by Arnold Myers, he was a welcome sight.

Richie led them into Pop's cozy living room while he prepared hot chocolate for everyone in the kitchen. As he waved them over to a small couch, Richie caught Thomas glancing at his black gloves.

"I've taken ill with a wretched cold ever since setting foot in this damp town of yours," he explained, with a kindly smile. "And quite aware that I would be expected to shake hands with so many people at the funeral, I decided to do my bit to keep from spreading harmful germs."

While Richie finished his preparations for the hot chocolates in the kitchen, Thomas and Jeni took turns chewing out Arnold for unleashing his "grand finale."

"Well, what if it had really been the Sieve?" he argued, not giving an inch. "Huh? What then? You would have owed me big time for saving your pansy as—"

"Is everything all right in there?" Richie called from the kitchen. "You didn't get smoke inhalation from all those explosives?"

"No! We're fine!" Jeni called back.

Thomas cast Arnold a sour look. But just before he was going to further chastise Arnold, telling him an exact place on his body where he could shove his "grand finale" next time, he caught sight of a picture on Pop's side table. It was a picture of Pop and Richie wearing scuba gear on the back of a fishing boat. Richie looked younger, his skin lightly tanned—probably due to being out on the water somewhere far away from the perpetual gloom of Gloomsbury. Diamonds of light danced across the water in the background. It was strangely comforting to see a photo of Pop alive and smiling after seeing him on the cooling board only a day before.

Richie's soft voice brought Thomas back to the room. A cup of steaming hot chocolate from a gloved hand was held out to Thomas. He took the cup happily while Richie handed mugs to Jeni and Arnold and took a seat by the fireplace. After a long silence punctuated by Arnold's slurps, Richie folded his black-gloved fingers together and said:

"So are you going to tell me why you three were snooping around my uncle's basement, hmm?"

Looking up from his steaming mug, Thomas suddenly had the strange feeling he was sitting on the couch of some psychologist who could peer into his brain and dissect every pattern of thought.

"I can imagine you have a thousand more fun things to do than poke around a moldy basement after a funeral," Richie continued. "It'd have to be pretty important, I'd say."

Jeni was about to come up with a famous Jeni Myers lie when she shifted her weight on the couch, spilling her hot chocolate.

She jerked up from the couch as if stung by a bee.

"Ouch!" Jeni cried, rubbing her arm.

Everyone saw it—including Richie.

Pop's diary had slipped from the folds of Jeni's black sweater and lay open on the floor.

"What do we have here?" said Richie, reaching down to pluck the book from the ground. He sat back down in his chair and idly thumbed through the pages. But then something caught his eye and he looked up suddenly.

"So Pop was following this group," he said.

"The Seeve," Arnold contributed excitedly. Jeni and Thomas both glared at him.

"*Sieve*, like give," Richie corrected, holding a gloved finger to his beard. "Like your mind, my boy."

"What?" said Arnold looking at Jeni. Jeni shook her head.

"Not important," said Richie, smiling again. "What *is* important is that my dear uncle truly thought that there were madmen from beyond the grave haunting your little town. Are you sure he didn't get into the communion wine?"

"Don't say that!" Thomas shouted. "Pop died because he found out what these guys were doing!"

"And what were they doing exactly, my friend?" Richie asked. "All we have is a description of some strange characters in black hats and glasses. Don't you think it's a little suspicious if an entire group of men were to wear—EVERYBODY GET DOWN!" he cried suddenly, leaping to his feet. "Quickly, in the kitchen, all of you!" he rasped in a hushed voice.

Thomas and Jeni flew to the kitchen, Arnold right behind them.

"What is it?" Jeni whispered.

"Somebody's outside, I think," Thomas whispered. "I can't tell. Maybe it's the Sieve."

Beneath the back door, a few fingers of fog began to make their way into the room. Arnold's eyes widened.

"Um...are you guys seeing this?" Arnold mumbled.

Without thinking, Thomas reached into his pocket, slowly withdrawing the wire-rimmed spectacles.

Jeni slapped his hand.

"Don't...do...that," Jeni hissed through clenched teeth.

For what seemed like an eternity Thomas, Jeni, and Arnold huddled in the priest's kitchen, until finally the front door swung open and Richie stumbled in, wiping his brow with a handkerchief from his pocket. The fingers of fog withdrew from under the door and disappeared back into the yard.

"Forgive me for not believing you," said Richie, dabbing sweat from his temples. "One of those men...the ones you described...in bowler hats was watching the house! I chased him down the street until he disappeared around a corner. We can't stay here much longer, I'm afraid."

"So you believe now Pop wasn't crazy?' said Thomas. "That he was murdered?"

"I do," said Richie in a quiet voice. "We have to recover whatever Pop found before these Sieve characters get their hands on it. I suggest we do a bit more digging. I'll go see if I can find anything in the church archives...I'll say it's a memorial piece for my late uncle. Let's meet tomorrow at Parishioner's Walk at noon and exchange intel. Agreed?"

Thomas looked at Jeni. *Did Richie just use a spy word?* Jeni smiled back at him and nodded her head as if she was thinking the same thing.

"Agreed," said Thomas.

"Now go!" said Richie. "Get home quick before any more of those monsters come knocking!"

They left Richie standing in the doorway of the cottage, the weird fingered fog curling out from under the garden bushes. Once they were across the street and out of sight, Jeni pulled Pop's diary from the folds of her black sweater.

"You stole Pop's diary?" Arnold asked, looking more shocked than if Sparky's Online Fireworks Bonanza had notified his parents of his outstanding balance.

"I didn't steal it. I just borrowed it," Jeni said defensively, flipping through the pages until she came to the one she was looking for. "Look!" she exclaimed triumphantly, her finger landing on a series of small numbers written in one corner of the book and easily overlooked…that is, if you didn't happen to be Jeni Myers.

"Forty-three longitude by fifty-nine latitude," Thomas read, peering through his glasses.

"They're coordinates," said Jeni. "Remember you overheard the Sieve outside your house whispering about the priest having the location? This is the location!"

"Let me see that," said Thomas taking the diary. "Yeah, but the coordinates are incomplete. They list everything except whether it is north, south, east, or west. Without these geographical parameters the numbers are useless."

"Jago parma what?" said Arnold.

Ignoring Arnold's blathering, Jeni took a rubber band from her wrist and tied up her hair. "I know that," she said. "I'm not an idiot, professor. Still, we're closer. I still don't trust that Richie guy, though. That whole running-around business outside? That was totally an act."

"It wasn't an act, Jen," said Thomas. "You saw the fog coming through the back door. It was real. Even Arnold saw it. Anyway, I gotta get home," said Thomas, glancing at his watch.

"So do we," said Jeni. "I'm gonna go over Pop's diary tonight. As soon I find anything out, I'll e-mail you. Be careful, Thomas."

"You too," he said.

Jeni yanked Arnold by the arm. Thomas could hear their argument all the way down the block. "Why do you always have to set off fireworks *inside* the house?" Jeni demanded.

"It's my trademark move," Arnold shot back. "Everybody needs one."

Mary Looks at Caesar

VII

Mary Looks at Caesar

Thomas pushed past the creaking front door and stepped into the foyer. He had steeled his nerves all the way down Thayer, preparing himself for another lecture full of shaming recriminations from Elijah Creeper the Fifth. Instead, he found the foyer empty and a note from his father lying on the table by the Creeper diary.

> Elijah Thomas,
> I am headed to a conference today in New York. While I am away I trust that you will see to it that your tasks are completed on schedule and to the best of your abilities. . . .

There were a few words after *abilities* but they were scratched out. It was as if his father had wanted to say more on the subject but changed his mind at the last minute, for which Thomas was grateful.

> Though I will not be here to check off your daily work, by now I trust we've come to an understanding about what is satisfactory and what is not. In the event of a delivery, Mort Shulling, who helped us when I had my gall bladder removed as you will recall, is on call to assist you.
> Make sure your mother eats something.

Thomas crumpled the note into a ball and threw it on the floor. He peered down the hallway to the kitchen door, which had been propped open. His mother sat motionless at the kitchen table, her back to the door, just as she had been when he left the house. *He should go and talk to her*, he thought.

It was what a good son would do, not a son who hated his life as Thomas did, and who confessed at particularly miserable times that he didn't like his parents much, either. It was a horrible, worthless feeling. But it hung around, like a cold in his heart.

An hour later, sprawled on his bed, munching on Stroher's hard pretzels, he carefully fished out the enchanted glasses from his pocket.

He regarded them now as a highly dangerous item—like a pair of snake fangs that still held a drop of venom, or a device that could be used to trigger a bomb. He turned the eyeglasses over in the lamplight, examining them closely. They seemed ordinary enough, with their round lenses and wire-rimmed frames. They were clearly from a different time period for sure, but didn't seem all that *magical* at first glance. Feeling strangely drowsy, his mind started to wander…

Then a beep from his iPhone announced a new e-mail. The sound startled him awake. His own glasses lay in his lap, and he had just been about to put the enchanted, wire-rimmed spectacles on his nose. He didn't even remember taking them off or deciding to put the magic ones on. He shivered, then placed the enchanted spectacles on the far side of his dresser table.

Swiping the iPhone screen, he brought up the e-mail app. A message from Jeni waited in his inbox. The subject line was typed in capital letters URGENT! PLEASE READ! I'M SERIOUS, PROFESSOR!

> I hope you get this tonight! I was right to grab the diary. There's a whole section that's written in cipher! Looks like Pop was even more paranoid than us.
>
> I can't crack it, Thomas. Please! I need your help!
>
> There's a riddle at the top of the page before the cipher. It says: *Mary QS stares at Caesar: Eyes open, Lips closed.* I looked it up. Mary QS must be Mary

> Queen of Scots and we all know who Caesar was. But what do you make of the second part? What does it matter if Mary's eyes are open and her lips closed?
>
> I know you are probably as tired as I am, but we need to figure it out before we meet that weirdo tomorrow. Do you think you can do it?
>
> Write me back as soon as you know anything.
>
> Jeni
>
> P.S. My parents found Arnold's firework stash—well, one of them. Looks like he's grounded. It's just you and me. Probably safer that way anyway LOL.

Thomas looked across the bed at Moses. The cat yawned and fell on its back, its paws spread-eagled in the air. He was all alone in solving the cipher. He chomped two more pretzels, cracked his fingers, and started to examine the encryption.

Mary QS stares at Caesar: Eyes open, Lips closed.

> Asvomrk xskixliv, Wriih erh Gviitiv jsyrh e aietsr xs hijiex Xli Wmizi. Jievmrk jsv xlimv pmziw, xlic higmhih xs fyvc mx sr xli fsxxsq sj xli sgier jpssv. Xlex mw alc Xli Wmizi wxmpp leyrx Kpssqwfyvc. Xlic evi zyprivefpi ew psrk ew Xli Aietsr ibmwxw erh tevesrsmh mx qec fi jsyrh erc hec. Alsqiziv xlic wywtigx, xlic ivehmgexi. Yrhiv kviex hyviiw M lezi psgexih xli viwxmrk tpegi sj Xli Aietsr…
>
> Espcp td l ueej dslapo wtvp l mlnvhlcod n l slwq xtwp qczx dszcp. Esp pilne nzzcotyled xlj mp qzfyo ty estd otlcj. Tq dzxpestyr slaayd ez xp, oz ld zfc qzcpqlespcd oto: dppv esp Yzceshpde Alddlrp.

It wasn't hard to figure out the part in Pop's riddle about Caesar. Thomas remembered from his reading that the Roman leader had been famous for sending encrypted messages back and forth from the front during times of war. The Roman commanders would use small circular devices that could rotate the encrypted letter to reveal the decrypted counterpart once they knew Caesar's cipher.

They had even named a cipher after Caesar—the "Caesar Shift." It was obvious that Pop was using a Caesar Shift in his diary since he mentioned Caesar's name in the riddle. But what was the other part about Mary Queen of Scots?

He opened the internet browser. He knew that most of the stuff he read online was full of holes and that you couldn't trust everything you read. He had to consider the source of the information, after all. But there was one credible website on ciphers and codes that might be able to shed light on Pop's riddle: Dr. Funk's Funky Code Junction.

Dr. Funk was a retired professor from University of Chicago, where he'd taught linguistics for over forty years. In retirement he'd become obsessed with encryption. He even became a bit of an internet celebrity, traveling the country, visiting high schools and corporate functions where he would challenge guests to give him an unbreakable cipher that he would miraculously decipher right in front of them.

Thomas always switched off the sound whenever he logged on to the website because it played a loop of this cheesy horn section with Dr. Funk's thick German voice shouting, "Think your code is unbreakable? I DON'T THINK SO!" Thomas scrolled through the website's menu until he found the section he was looking for: "Famous Cryptologists Now in the Crypt." A new window flashed open. He scrolled down until he came to "Caught Red-Handed," a section on cryptologists who had been caught in the act of espionage and met bloody ends. When he came across the name of Mary Queen of Scots his eyes lit up. As it turned out, Mary Queen of Scots had used the Caesar Shift cipher to communicate with members of her inner circle. But she'd modified the traditional cipher with a few quirks here and there, varying the pattern throughout the message.

That was it! he realized. *Mary QS stares at Caesar.* Pop's diary entry was a modified Caesar Shift!

Brimming with excitement, Thomas turned back to the page. He chewed at his lower lip. *The quirk was there, right under his nose.* He examined the text back and forth. Pop had capitalized certain letters. The *M* and *C* of Mary and Caesar, which made sense, thought Thomas. Proper names were always capitalized. But why then were the E and the L in *Eyes open, Lips closed?* The encrypted text of the cipher underneath looked like a lump of jumbled word spaghetti. But two lines formed a separate paragraph. *What if,* he thought, feeling his pulse start to spike. *What if...?*

He grabbed his pencil and wrote out the two ciphers: first, the *E* cipher where *A* became *E*, so on and so forth, until he rotated through all twenty-six letters of the alphabet. Then he wrote out the *L* cipher where *A* became *L*. Even if the person who stumbled upon the diary deciphered the first paragraph, if they didn't know the quirky little twist at the end, the message would remain incomplete.

E	I = M	R = V
A = E	J = N	S = W
B = F	K = O	T = X
C = G	L = P	U = Y
D = H	M = Q	V = Z
E = I	N = R	W = A
F = J	O = S	X = B
G = K	P = T	Y = C
H = L	Q = U	Z = D

L	I = T	R = C
A = L	J = U	S = D
B = M	K = V	T = E
C = N	L = W	U = F
D = O	M = X	V = G
E = P	N = Y	W = H
F = Q	O = Z	X = I
G = R	P = A	Y = J
H = S	Q = B	Z = K

With his two ciphers written out, Thomas started working through the text using the *E* cipher for the first part. As the words started to emerge with each pencil stroke, he knew his suspicions had been right.

He had deciphered the secret message.

> Working together, Sneed and Creeper found a weapon to defeat the Sieve. Fearing for their lives, they decided to bury it on the ocean floor. That is why the Sieve still haunt Gloomsbury. They are vulnerable as long as The Weapon exists and paranoid it may be found any day. Whomever they suspect, they eradicate. Under great duress I have located the resting place of The Weapon....

Thomas switched over to the *L* cipher and took a deep breath. This was it, he thought, the secret resting place of the Weapon that Sneed and Elijah Creeper the First had placed in the boat. His fingers trembled as he wrote out the final words. He held the paper up to his nose in the pale lamplight, his whole body shaking like Frankenstein's creature after being jolted by raw electricity.

> There is a jetty shaped like a backwards c a half mile from shore. The exact coordinates may be found in this diary. If something happens to me, do as our forefathers did: seek the Northwest Passage.

Northwest Passage was underlined. It was right there in black and white: North and West.

The missing coordinates!

Thomas took several photos of the decrypted message with his iPhone. He had to do several shots because his hands were shaking so badly. Finally, when he had a clear photo, he sent it to Jeni. He felt like a hero, and though he knew it was just a small victory, he felt like cheering. They had a chance now.

They had a chance to defeat the Sieve.

He put the iPhone under his pillow and switched off the light. He looked at his digital watch in the darkness. It was almost one-thirty in the morning. *How long had he been working at the cipher? An hour? Two hours?* He couldn't say. Time had fallen away like smoke from a fire. Exhaustion crept through his bones, his pulse slowed, and his breath came in a steady rhythm. Sometime later, just before his eyelids closed, he took off his glasses and placed them on his dresser. He yawned and turned over onto his side. The last thing he thought before he sank into velvet folds of sleep was that Jeni was going to be so proud of him.

❧

Thomas awoke to the sound of birds chirping in the oak tree outside his window.

His mouth felt parched, and he was desperate for a sip of water. Blindly, he fumbled for his glasses and swung his feet to the cold floor. As he approached the door of his room, he came to a dead stop.

Fingers of fog gathered around his feet. The fingers reached up, turning the doorknob for him. Thomas gasped. The door swung open into a hallway filled with swirling fog. His heart sank to the creaking floorboards. He had put on the wrong glasses.

He tried to remove the glasses from his nose, but this time the fog fought back. The curling fingers were like freezing lassos. They wrapped tightly about his arms until he couldn't shake loose their hold. The fog was in control, and it pushed him across the hall to the room. David's old room. Thomas tried to call for help, but the fog covered his mouth with numbing fingers. He was helpless.

Once inside David's room the fog released him, swirling back from Thomas's limbs to slam the door behind him. Whirling around, he tugged frantically on the knob but the fog gummed up the hinges and the keyhole, holding the door fast, sealing it up like the pressurized door on a submarine.

Thomas heard the soft, lightning-fast clicks of a keyboard behind him and turned around in horror. David was bending over his laptop, the light from the laptop screen bathing his face in an eerie glow.

"David?" Thomas whispered. But David paid no attention to him. Like Elijah the First, David couldn't hear or see him. Thomas moved to David's side. His brother's face was drawn up in a tight mask of fear. Thomas looked down at the computer screen. He read the words on the screen out loud, but in the alternate, dream-like world of the enchanted glasses the words came echoing back to him slower and stranger, as if he were calling from the bottom of a well.

> There is a horrible secret in Gloomsbury! I can't tell Father about it even though he will know soon enough because I'm afraid I've led them right to our doorstep.
>
> I first saw one of the Sieve by the rocks of the old quarry outside of town. It wore a strange black hat, and seemed to sense my presence because it followed me home. I fear they are watching me now. I've seen several of them waiting at night on the other side of the road in an old black car. What are they waiting for? Why are they watching me? I'm afraid to tell anyone. I think anyone who notices them is in danger.

David stopped typing and closed the laptop. Sliding into bed, he closed his eyes. He tossed and turned for a few moments before getting up to open the bedroom window. He crawled back under the sheets and closed his eyes. Thomas crouched by David's bedside, trying to wake him, but like when he had visited the Dyre Dunes, he was a ghost to this world, to this past time. *Why didn't you tell me?* Thomas wanted to shout as his eyes filled with tears. *I would have helped you! Why did you keep this secret? I was your friend too, David. Remember! I was your friend. . . .*

Then Thomas heard a screeching against the windowpane. The fog had returned and was swirling wildly around his ears.

"No!" Thomas shouted as long yellow nails appeared out of the darkness, scratching across the windowpane. Like the spiky legs on a crab, the nails fanned up under the gap between the window and windowsill and jerked the window open. Out of the fog a wiry black body pulled itself through the window to crouch at the headboard. The sickly, pale face shone through the swirling fog—eyes milk-white, devoid of any color or pupil, the mouth a jagged grin of loose flesh over stained, chipped teeth. Thomas tried to rush forward but the fog clamped its cold fingers around his ankles like chains.

"Stay…away…from him!" Thomas shouted, the sound of his voice echoing through the room in the slow dream-like language as before. "Get…out of…here!" A raspy, dry voice echoed through Thomas's mind:

You are not supposed to be here! Where did you get those? Tell me! A long white finger, its yellow nail curved and sharp like a dagger, stabbed at him. The voice in his head changed from a whisper to a roar. *I SAID, WHERE DID YOU GET THOSE GLASSES, LITTLE MORTICIAN?*

Suddenly, David jolted awake. His eyes grew wide with terror seeing the demented face hovering over him. But before he could even scream, the grinning man reached down and put his white claw-like hand over David's heart. The room exploded with wild light. Thomas fell backwards onto the floor

"STOP!" Thomas yelled, thrashing his hands. "DON'T TOUCH HIM!"

Out of the swirling fog, something small and white reached out and flung the glasses off Thomas's nose. He felt his body jerk up into the accelerating wormhole of mist as the dark bedroom fell away beneath him, replaced a second later by a blurry white ceiling. He was in his own room again. But something was wrong. There was still a death-chill wafting over him.

Thomas looked up. Silvie Creeper stood over him holding out her hand. Hovering in the center of the ghost's pale palm were the enchanted glasses. Thomas watched in awe as Silvie raised her palm and moved her hand toward a desk drawer. The enchanted glasses rose into the air and swept over to the drawer, which opened gently to receive them. With a quick flick of Silvie's undead wrist, the drawer snapped shut.

"Silvie, how did you…?" Thomas stammered. He blinked and reached up and grabbed his glasses, the safe and non-magic kind, from his bed. "You know…magic?" he whispered.

A few small spells. That's how the magician first got me into the tent at Town Beach. Fingal and I were part of his show. You shouldn't be messing around with those glasses, Thomas. They're bad. Really bad.

Thomas was about to reply that he didn't mean to "mess around" with anything, when the glowing form of a dog came bounding out of Thomas's closet. A wild green luminescence shimmered all around the massive animal. The green ghost-dog gave Thomas's head a few wet and chilly licks (which, if you've ever been licked by a ghost dog, feels exactly like someone wiping frosty soft-serve ice cream against your cheek). He stared in amazement at the panting, glowing animal, its large, furry face and muscular body more like a giant wolf than any dog he had ever seen.

Fingal's getting impatient, Thomas, said Silvie. *We both are. You need to solve this mystery so I can get my arm back. You owe me.*

Silvie Creeper smiled at the supernatural ghost-dog who watched Thomas with a wolfish grin.

Fingal likes you! That's good. Now, you need to get a move on, Thomas. I've found something that might help you, an old watch that used to belong to your great-great-grandfather. But first you must talk with your mother, Thomas. Make things right. A glimmer of sadness passed over Silvie Creeper's dark eyes. *I'd give anything to talk to my mother again.*

Then, without any warning, the two ghosts were gone. Thomas was alone again, sitting on the floor in the dark.

But he could hear the whisper retreating in his mind like a secret wind rustling away:

Do it for me!

ALDOUS

VIII

"Not in That Much Pain"

It was true, Thomas had steered clear of his mother in recent months. At the end of the school year, instead of some great graduation gift, his parents had dropped the bombshell that he would not be attending Gloomsbury High School in the fall with the rest of his classmates. From ninth grade on, he would be homeschooled at Creeper & Sons.

They believed—although Thomas knew his father was the one pulling the strings—that it would make the eventual transition to full-time management of the funeral home easier. His father would handle all instruction in funereal science, while his mother, a former English teacher, would take over "the useless padding required by the state to mold a child into an incompetent clod of uselessness and entitlement" (a direct quote from Elijah Creeper the Fifth).

Thomas wasn't sure which one of his parents infuriated him more. It was harder to take out that anger on his father because it was like throwing gasoline on an already well-stoked fire. In the end, he punished his mother with the only weapon he had at his command: silence. But that morning, thinking of Silvie's plea to make amends with his mother, he descended the long staircase, prepared to have the first non-monosyllabic conversation with his mother in months.

He found her in the Viewing Room. She was busy frantically vacuuming the carpet, and although the bag was bulging with overstuffed dust and cobwebs, she didn't seem to notice. The smell of stale cigarette smoke wafted in the open window. It was Sunday, which meant Jed would be smoking on the porch, waiting for his friend Mr. Green to arrive from

Atlantic City with Jed's "payout" from whatever recent get-rich-quick scheme they had cooked up. Glancing up, Mrs. Creeper finally noticed her son standing in the doorway.

"Hi, sweetie," his mother said, clicking off the vacuum cleaner.

"Hey," said Thomas. He could see the crumpled paper in his mother's pocket—one of her endless to-do lists. There was so much that needed doing in the old house, so many tasks to check off, an endless highway of lists stretching out to the gloomy horizon. Looking at his mother, Thomas couldn't fight the feeling he was watching his mother disappear, little by little, dissolving into her duties.

"Dad said I'm supposed to get you to eat something," he said. "Why don't we go to Sappy's for breakfast? I think I'd like to get out of the house. It's not raining too hard. We could walk."

"Yes, dear. That is a marvelous idea," Mrs. Creeper exclaimed. "I just need…to grab something. I'll meet you outside in two minutes."

❧

Sappy's was the kind of diner whose name articulated its décor to a perfect *T*.

The sinking building looked like a hat someone had mistakenly sat on. It was sandwiched between the town post office and a brick building that had once operated as a courthouse before it collapsed unexpectedly into a giant sinkhole five years before. Mayor Plugg, who at that time had been a councilman-at-large (large having a double meaning in that Plugg weighed over three hundred fifty pounds) made it one of his initiatives to rebuild the old courthouse after its sinkhole debacle. But as soon as Plugg was elected to the office of mayor, the drive to rebuild stalled, just as all bright ideas got slowed and arrested by the town's depressing gloom. Today, as Thomas and his mother passed by, nothing had changed. The site of the former courthouse was still a mountain of loose bricks, cordoned off by a large chain-link fence hung with several KEEP OUT signs. So much for great initiatives.

Thomas and Mrs. Creeper pushed through the revolving door and stepped into the deserted diner—deserted save for a man Thomas recognized as that of the fellow who had dumped his cat out on the window ledge at the Fisherman's Haven Hotel during the sun sighting. He seemed to have made amends with his cat, who sat beside him in the booth, licking its paws. The old sea-dog caught Thomas looking his way and flashed him a toothless scowl.

Thomas and his mother placed their order, then sat in awkward silence for some time. While Thomas tried to think of what to say and how to say it, Mrs. Creeper withdrew a small package from her purse.

"It's the strangest thing," she said, placing the package on the tabletop. "I meant to give this to you for Christmas." She paused and pursed her colorless lips. "Did we do Christmas this year?

"Yep," Thomas lied. Clearly, throwing a joyous Christmas occasion must not have made it on any of his mother's many to-do lists.

"Oh," said Mrs. Creeper absently. "I'm sorry, Thomas. I have trouble remembering things sometimes. There's this confusion in my head sometimes…like a fog. I just can't seem to—"

"Mom," said Thomas, reaching out to take his mom's hand in his own. "I know it's hard without David—" he began. "We never talk about him."

Mrs. Creeper's face crumpled in anguish. Thomas let go of her hand and yanked a wad of napkins from the dispenser as tears rolled down his mother's face.

"It just doesn't make sense," she sobbed. "David was… so strong."

"I know," said Thomas, swallowing hard. "I just can't live…like he's a ghost we don't talk about."

"You're right," Mrs. Creeper managed with a weak smile,

wiping the tears from her cheeks with the sides of the napkin. She seemed to brighten a little, and Thomas was reminded that his mother was still in there somewhere. *She* was like a ghost in the house too, he realized. *What was her Artifact of Unlocking?* Silvie was right. Talking about the pain seemed to change his mother. Maybe words were like Artifacts of Unlocking. Maybe speaking the unexplainable and the terrible out loud—putting that fear and pain outside the mind so you could see it more clearly—maybe that was its own kind of unlocking.

Mrs. Creeper blew her nose and balled the napkin into her purse. She flashed another smile and moved the package across the table to Thomas.

"Go on! Open it!" she said, flashing a rare beam of joy. "I think it belonged to your namesake…Elijah Thomas Creeper the First. I found it a year ago while putting away winter clothes in the attic, and I know how you like old devices and spy stuff from those books you read."

Thomas unwrapped the package slowly, the pages of newspaper crackling like mummy skin. It was a gleaming pocket watch. The outer casing was made of brass, and there were well-worn spots where thumbs and fingers had clutched it all those years ago. A small ink drawing of an owl sat atop the number twelve. Above the owl's head the name of the watchmaker was inscribed in sloping, black letters: **ALDOUS**

"It's self-winding," said Mrs. Creeper. "It has its own stopwatch you can adjust. I think it still works."

"Thank you," said Thomas. "I love it."

The waiter deposited two plates on the table, piled high with stacks of blueberry pancakes, several sausages, a pile of crisp bacon, and two sides of sizzling hash browns. Thomas had secretly ordered double, knowing his mother would ask for only a cup of coffee. Making sure his mother ate had been on his "list" left by his father. And unlike Santa, Thomas knew his father checked his list more than twice.

He placed the antique watch in his pants pocket and pushed a plate of food closer to his mother.

"Sorry," said Thomas smiling faintly. "I promised Dad."

Mrs. Creeper smiled back and took up her fork.

"Don't know why," she said, shaking her head as she picked at a plate of hash browns. "I just don't have much of an appetite these days. Must be the weather."

"Must be," said Thomas.

After breakfast they returned home. While the Creepers weren't known for being affectionate or saying I love you, Thomas felt that it had been a happy morning, that something had thawed between his mother and him. The top layer of ice on a pond can still get warm in the sun, he thought, even in the dead of winter.

Thomas raced through his chores, then headed up the rickety staircase to his bedroom. As a heavy rain began to pelt against his window, he set about making final preparations for his meeting with Jeni and Richie. He loaded his backpack with essential supplies: Uncle Percival's penknife and the enchanted wire-rimmed spectacles; a few smoke bombs; and a lighter Jeni had stolen from Arnold's stash—great for creating a diversion should they need one.

Lastly, he threw in Elijah Creeper the First's pocket watch that Silvie had somehow brought to his mother's attention.

He checked his Ken Darby Spy Watch. He smiled. Just enough time to get to Parishioner's Walk. He was right on time.

❧

A few minutes after twelve, Thomas arrived at the old stone courtyard known as Parishioner's Walk. Located directly behind Gloomsbury Cemetery, it was an eerie place even in the daylight, with moss-covered flagstones and tall pillars strangled by ivy. The courtyard itself—which had once served as the grounds for church *fêtes*, gatherings, and games for children—was flanked by rows of dismal-looking trees with scrawny branches that never seemed to produce either leaf or bud. At night, looming with shadows and wrapped in mist, the courtyard was positively terrifying. To make matters worse, there was the troubling issue of scabber weed.

Scabber weed was one of Gloomsbury's most peculiar phenomena, which grew in wide swaths across hillsides or festered in cracks between cobblestone and brick. (This pernicious weed—and pernicious, in case you didn't know, means thoroughly dreadful—thrives on mold, decay, and darkness, all of which Gloomsbury had in plenty). Mayor Plugg had launched a campaign the previous year to combat the town's infamous scabber weed infestation. But like all his initiatives, the effort was short-lived. It was a losing battle. Scabber weed grew in dense tendrils, perfectly suited to trip up feet and create a nasty rash on exposed ankles and shins. Scabber weed particularly relished the dark and gloomy confines of Parishioner's Walk—indeed, the residents had come to believe this spot as the noxious plant's ancestral home.

Thomas wiped the rain from his glasses and glanced around the deserted courtyard. There was no sign of Jeni. *Maybe she was running late*, he thought. The courtyard in front of Thomas, shadowed here and there by patches of scabber weed, ended in a small stone staircase that led through a series of trails that wound down toward the ocean. Thomas pulled his socks up over his pant legs. As he stepped gingerly from stone to stone, making his way to the staircase, he could see the dark swirl of the sea through the leafless branches. At the top of the staircase he stopped short.

A high-pitched wail reverberated through the forest.

It was a girl's voice. *A girl screaming....*

He flew down the staircase, nearly losing his balance again, and leapt over a nest of scabber weed (it had festered to twice its size since Thomas had last laid eyes on it). Wet branches slapped at his face as he ran, but he batted them away. Heading too fast down one side of the trail he tripped.

He gnashed his teeth as the stinging tendrils wrapped around his wrist. He fought free of their grip and clambered back to his feet. *Get yourself together,* he told himself. *You're not going to be of any use to anyone if you panic and lose your head like an idiot.*

He made it down to a small clearing, where he skidded to a halt, his heart dropping like a lead anchor into his belly. Jeni was up ahead in the clearing.

And one of the Sieve had her by the throat.

Tell us! Tell us! Tell us! a chorus of raspy voices cried in Thomas's brain. *Where is the location, boy? Tell us!*

"Thomas!" Jeni shouted.

Thomas made it a few steps closer. Jeni's eyes widened as the arm around her neck began to change. The skin became slowly incandescent, pulsing with the wild, fluorescent light. The surface of the Sieve's glowing arm began to squirm. Thomas watched Jeni's face drain of all color. Her eyes froze, her body slumping toward the ground.

"Stop it!" Thomas cried. "Let go of her!"

But his words came back to him twisted and distorted in the whispery language of the Sieve: *Stopppppppp it! Let gooooooo of her!*

Thomas reached for the penknife in his pocket. But before he could pull it out, the Sieve snarled and hauled Jeni's limp body off into the tangle of trees, bushes, and festering scabber weed.

Thomas flew after them, rain streaming across his glasses, obscuring his field of vision. The Sieve had moved off the trail, into the denser thicket. Thomas fought his way, wincing through the thorny shrubbery and scabber weed patches, following the light of the Sieve's arm until it disappeared into the forest gloom.

He gasped. *Where did they go?* He scanned the descending forest, heart racing. *There!* The light of the arm appeared again, several yards down. Thomas flew toward the light, nearly falling down into a giant sinkhole that had been concealed by fallen branches. And suddenly the pieces fell together in Thomas's mind, the clues he had picked up along the way without even realizing it:

The Sieve traveled through the sinkholes!

He watched the wild light disappear and reappear through the scabber weed below. They were nearing a cliff overlooking the sea tossed with whitecaps. Determined to find a faster way down, Thomas slid down a gully surging with the cold rush of recent rain. While it had seemed an ingenious way to get down quickly, the water was flowing too fast, and the cliff was just ahead. If he couldn't stop himself, he'd go over the side!

Thomas flailed out like a blind man grasping for something—anything to stop his headlong flight. Closing his eyes tightly, he thought of Jeni, his parents, David. He prayed that whatever happened, Jeni would somehow get free of the Sieve, and his body wouldn't be eaten by the great white sharks that patrolled the bay....

"Gotcha!"

Two strong hands grabbed his collar and pulled him up from the wet rush of water, just inches from the precipice. Thomas stared up through fogged-over glasses: white face, blond beard, floppy gray hat.

Richie Mulvaney.

"C'mon," said Richie, brushing a few wet leaves off Thomas's shoulder. "Jeni doesn't have much time. This way!"

Weak-kneed and shaken from his near-death encounter, Thomas stumbled after Richie down another gully until it bottomed out at the beachhead. A wet bar of sand stretched before them, waves rolling in past barnacled jetties littered with the droppings of sea birds. A thick cattail marsh stretched out on either side, barely visible beneath a gathering fog. *Where was Jeni?* Thomas cupped his trembling hands around his mouth and shouted at the top of his lungs:

"Jeni!"

But there was no response, just the crashing surf and the

screeching of gulls in the distance. Then he noticed the footprints: two sets tracking down from the sand toward the surf. But in the white spume at the edge of the water the tracks disappeared. *Oh god,* thought Thomas. *No! No!*

He ran into the surf and scanned the waves as the fog swirled in thick and wild and the wind swept up, hissing through the cattails. He could hear Richie breathing heavily behind him; clearly he too was winded from their mad dash down from the forest.

"Jeni!" Thomas cried again.

But Jeni didn't answer. Another voice called out behind him as the fog sprouted fingers, curling menacingly around his ankles and wrists.

"Don't worry, little mortician," the dry voice behind his shoulder rasped. "She's not in that much pain. Not yet!"

Thomas whirled around. Like chips of paint falling from an old portrait, the face of Richie Mulvaney started to crumble. In the cracks behind the fake skin, white creatures wriggled, their tube-like bodies throbbing and pulsing with light. The air was sucked out of Thomas's lungs. The man—the same man from the photograph at the library and the east side of the cemetery—stepped forward, his decoy shell falling away piece by piece. The gray floppy hat warped in and out, as if by some foul spell. It grew smaller and darker until it settled on the man's rotting scalp in the form of the black bowler. Thomas backed away, his feet slipping in the shifting sand. But then he heard the sound of a motor sputtering through the surf. He turned and spied the bow of a wood-paneled motorboat cutting through the dense fog, which seemed to lift like a curtain to let the boat pass.

Jeni was standing at the bow. Her expression was blank, her eyes open wide but unmoving. The Sieve had her by the throat, the little wriggling creatures coming in and out of the rotten fingers like the writhing legs on a centipede. Thomas's heart sank. It was hopeless. There was nowhere to run.

"Didn't I warn you?" the man rasped behind him, a

wheezing cackle escaping his pale lips. "You could have left us alone! You could have gone in for milk and cookies! But now, Thomas Creeper, you must show us! You must show us what you've learned!"

Thomas reached for the penknife, but his hand felt sluggish and heavy. He slumped to his knees in the wet sand, the man towering over him—the false Richie, the one Jeni had suspected all along if only Thomas had believed her.

Thomas's head hit the sand. The man removed his black gloves, then slowly began to unroll his sleeves. There was no help coming, no protection from the living or dead that could help Thomas now. The claw came closer, the arm bursting with fluorescent light. The creatures inside the rotten flesh began to writhe wilder and wilder as the light swelled. Elijah Creeper the First had known it, right before he disappeared, leaving behind his enigmatic one-word note. Only now did Thomas understand, and the word was on his lips as the arm teeming with the disgusting creatures came closer into view, the field of light enveloping him and holding him in its paralyzing strobe:

Worms!

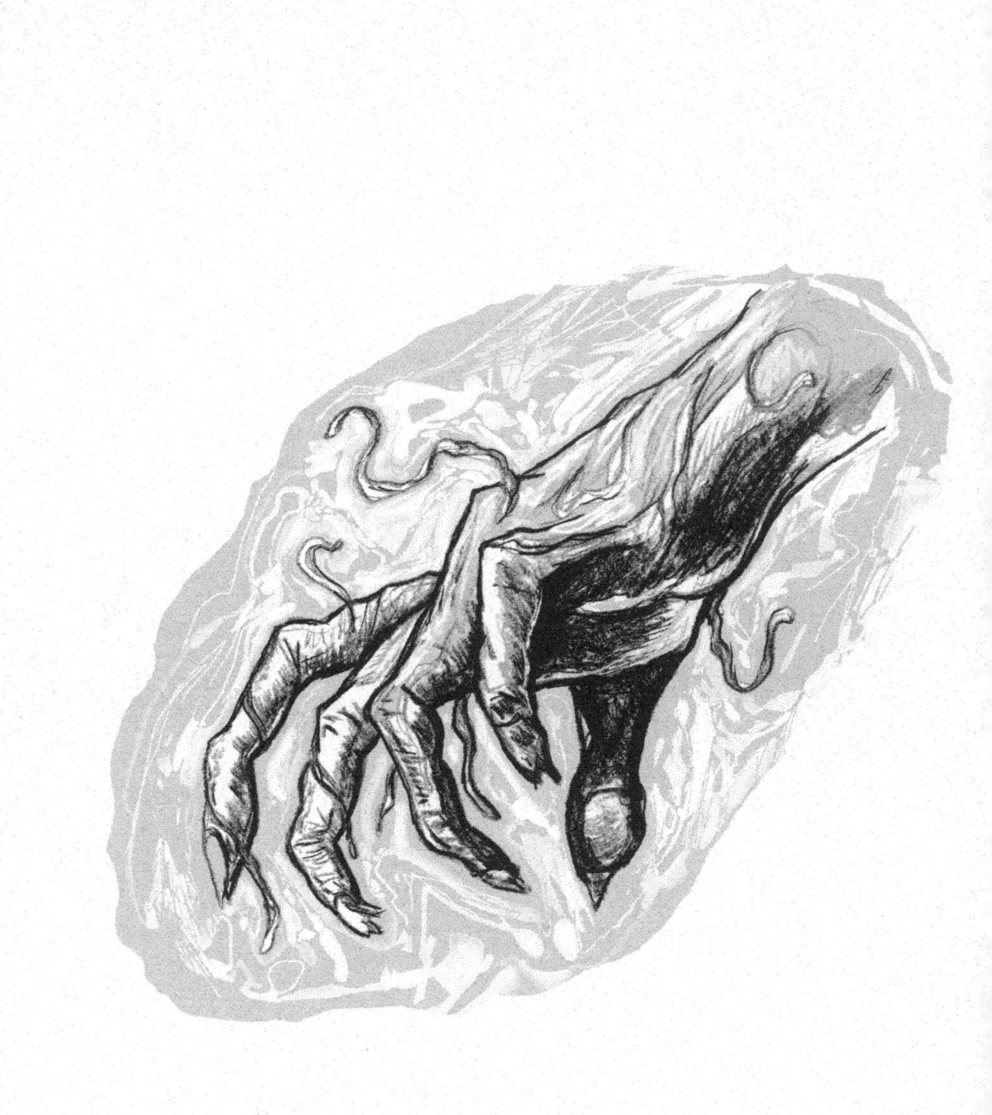

IX

As Constant and as Old As Time

As his eyes opened, little by little, Thomas hoped that the rocking feeling was just the old house creaking a little more than normal, that he was back in his bed and that everything that had happened had been the work of some wicked nightmare. He was wrong.

He was lying in the bottom of the boat. The wood seized and crackled slightly with every lift and descent. The air smelled rank and salty. He could feel the warmth of another body pressed up against his back. He tried to move his hands but they were tied behind him.

"Thomas! Wake up!"

It was Jeni! And she was alive! A bloom of joy rushed through him. He strained his fingers and reached out until he touched her hand and squeezed hard.

"Ah! Still with us?" a dry voice called out from somewhere in the rocking cabin. "Why, you do continue to amaze!"

Thomas turned his head. He could see the grinning man lounging on a large crate. He had changed his attire yet again. He now wore an impeccable black suit with a white linen shirt and a thin black tie, looped in an ornate fashion under the collar. His legs were neatly crossed, the black bowler resting in his lap. With one pale finger he circled the dusty brim of the hat. From the faint light of a small gas lamp swinging in the rafters Thomas could see the flesh on the crown of the man's head had all but rotted away, revealing the white dome of his skull.

"I thought since we had some time till we reached the

location, we might chat a bit. Thank you again, Ms. Myers, for providing us with the coordinates. Such willingness to help! Our little class *factotum*!"

"I'm sorry, Thomas," Jeni whispered over her shoulder. "They said they'd throw you overboard with your hands tied if I didn't tell them."

"Don't worry about it, Jen," said Thomas.

"As I was saying," the man continued, placing the bowler back on his head. "Now that we are locked into our destination—hook, line, and sinker, as it were!—and given that you have kindly provided our destination, I thought I might return the favor by filling in the gaps in your faulty research. It would be a shame, after all, if you met your untimely end wholly in the dark. I am not altogether a pitiless man, you know. But of course, where are my manners? We have not been formally introduced!"

Jumping to his feet and leaning down so that his rotting, receding gums were close to Jeni and Thomas's head, he made another small bow.

"You're Jacob M. Crowley," Jeni cried. "You're in that photograph in the library. The one Mr. Tolbert found, the one we weren't supposed to see after you disappeared. And that crate over there," Jeni added, motioning with her chin. "It says Property of Crowley's Trollers, East Barnstable, MA. Jacob M. Crowley, Proprietor."

"High marks, Jeni Myers! You *are* the smarter of the two," exclaimed Jacob Crowley. "And while I don't have an apple for you, I do have a little gift."

Grinning from ear to rotten ear, Crowley pulled a worm from his wrist and held it up above his head to examine it as one might a rare, forgotten fossil. The hand lowered toward Jeni, who cringed away, eyes wide with fear. Then it paused.

"But let's be fair!" said Crowley. "Mr. Creeper deserves another shot at the school prize. Tell me, little mortician, what do you find beneath the earth, beneath sand and stone? What is as constant and as old as the passage of time? You, who love riddles and puzzles above all things, should know the answer to this!"

Thomas looked away. He didn't want to play the game of some undead madman.

"Come now!" cried Crowley. "I'd think you of all people would jump at the chance of solving a great riddle! No?"

Crowley leaned down until his rotting nose was almost touching Thomas's cheek. The wretched smell of decay filled Thomas's nostrils, making him gasp for air.

"Then let me illuminate the dark for you, little mortician," rasped Crowley. "Let me show you what that fool of a priest never could figure out!" He dangled the worm in front of Thomas's face, the strange fluorescent light throbbing inside the wriggling body. "Do you see the glorious glow, Thomas Creeper? I wasn't the first to be infected, but I was the most changed afterwards. I was anointed, you see, given greater gifts than the others. The others, they are merely worker bees. While the infection rippled through my body, my thoughts remained my own. Would you like to know the story of how I became so anointed, so very powerful, Thomas Creeper?"

Crowley paused and lifted his rotting nose, sniffing the air like a dog.

"I still smell the salt air of the afternoon. We were desperate. Poor wretches from poor families that had no great New England names to cling to. Our destiny arrived one night within the most unremarkable crate, like so many others in the belly of the ship filled with tackle and dry goods. Unlike my wretched comrades, however, I could read. I had agreed to help a friend move a shipment of rum from the West Indies to Boston in exchange for a share in profits. The crate had traveled from the Far East, yet there was no mention of it in the ship's inventory logs. Our deckhand Benson, drunk on rum, took a crowbar to the crate, certain he'd find exotic jewels, silks, spices...perhaps something to trade for more swill. Instead we only found sacks full of limestone powder used in the manufacture of cement. But nesting within the powder, Thomas, hundreds of bright and luminous worms! They wriggled under our skin, into the cracks of our eyes. They showed us the path forward, whereby humanity may be transformed into something truly spectacular, blessed by immortality and above all, by ancient, sleepless magic. Observe!"

Crowley blew a stream of white fog from his lungs. The fog swirled around Thomas's neck like a noose, then disappeared. Another Sieve drone appeared, a worm dangling from between rotting fingertips, and reached down toward Jeni.

"Stop!" cried Thomas. "I'll help you! Don't hurt her!

"'Stop! Don't hurt her!'" Crowley mimicked. "But we can't stop, can we, Benson?"

The Sieve holding back Jeni's head grinned, worms writhing where his tongue used to be.

"Caaaaaaaan't!" hissed Benson. "Neverrrrr stopppppp!"

"Yes!" exclaimed Crowley, the light in his sunken eyes growing wilder and brighter. "We will change her and make her soft flesh ripple with immortal life! You shall see for yourself what you Creepers could have become had you not thrown in with those other meddlers, the Sneeds. You shall soon see, Thomas Creeper, what happens to those who resist our glorious enterprise! Once we locate and destroy the Weapon, all those we have marked and sent under we shall reawaken. No more hunger, no more rich or poor. No more of this rough business of life. Just the eternal present stretching out like a welcoming hand. . . ."

Crowley turned and lowered the wriggling worm down toward Jeni's face.

"Get. . .away from me. . .you zombie freak!" Jeni cried through gritted teeth. She tried to twist away, but Benson held her fast.

"*Tssk-tssk*," Crowley admonished. "'Zombie freak?' You are more articulate than that! Now, stay still! Open your mouth! When our little friend has done his duty, you shall experience pain like you've never felt before. The worms shall multiply within you, like a virus let loose within the walls of your chest...."

Benson forced open Jeni's mouth. His sharp nails dug into her cheeks until they drew blood.

"Stop it!" screamed Thomas.

The enchanted fog swirled from Crowley's mouth, circling around Thomas's face, pulling back his neck and eyelids.

"And I will make you watch, Thomas Creeper!" Crowley hissed, gnashing his cracked and stained teeth. "I will show you and all Creepers that you have failed. I will—"

CRACK!

The cabin lurched sideways.

Crates of buoys and mooring rigging flew from one side of the cabin to the other, as if the cabin were a snow globe shaken by a giant fist. From the deck above Thomas and Jeni heard a chorus of voices, rising in tone and pitch like a swarm of bees.

CRACK!

The cabin rolled violently again. Jeni tumbled into Thomas. Stumbling, Crowley dropped the worm. He sneered and held out his hand. Pointing to Thomas's feet, Thomas watched in horror as the worm changed directions, wriggling back across the floor, coming straight for him! But then there was water everywhere—cold salt water rushing in under his and Jeni's feet.

The ship was sinking.

"If the great white sharks don't pull you apart limb from limb," snarled Crowley. "Then we shall find you again, Thomas Creeper! Dead or alive, we shall find you!"

Crowley cast Jeni and Thomas one last wicked sneer, the light pulsing in his eyes, before he and his henchman Benson disappeared up the ladder in a flourish of swirling fog.

"Thomas!" shouted Jeni. "We gotta get out of here! The ship—"

"—is sinking!" Thomas yelled back. "Yeah, I figured that

one out. There's a penknife in my pocket! Hold on! I'll see if I can wedge it out!"

He fumbled for the penknife as the Sieve's discordant whispers rose in his ears.

"How do they do that?" Thomas shouted. "Get inside your brain like that?"

"I don't know!" Jeni barked back. "But I freakin' hate these guys!"

Twisting, Thomas eased the knife out of his pocket. The knife slipped from his fingers and rolled down beside the crate.

"Crap!" cried Thomas. "I dropped it! It's closer to you. Right there. Can you grab it?"

Jeni strained her back. Her fingers fluttered around until she grasped cold metal. "Got it!" she called out.

"Okay," said Thomas, wriggling closer to her. "Now try to cut the rope around my wrists."

Jeni positioned the blade and took a deep breath.

"Ouch! Careful!" Thomas cried. "Don't slit my wrists!"

"I'm trying my best!" shouted Jeni. The water was up to their chests now. The frigid chill was numbing Jeni's hands, making it harder to control the blade.

"Look, Jeni if we don't…" Thomas began, the water lapping against his neck and rising rapidly. "If we don't make it out I want to tell you…"

"Just a little…more!" she cried as the water reached her chin.

The underwater rope frayed, then split apart.

His arms freed, Thomas removed his glasses and stuffed them into his shirt pocket before they could get swept away. The world morphed before his eyes into blur of dark wood and rushing water. He could see Jeni's pale face. She held her head above the rushing water, gasping for breath.

"Hold your breath, Jeni!" Thomas shouted. I'm going to—"

Then he dropped the blade.

He watched it fall down through the water as the bow of the ship rose to a vertical position, as if they were on some demented theme-park ride. Thomas slipped beneath the water, salt water stinging his eyes. He caught a blurry glimpse of metal lying atop a crate and swam down to retrieve it. Then, bracing his feet on a porthole, he reached for Jeni, struggling to tread water. He cut the rope that held her wrists. Jeni's hands came free.

CRACK! CRACK!

A rush of seawater swept Thomas and Jeni up toward the bow and the last pocket of air left in the cabin.

"Thomas!" Jeni cried, flailing wildly as she batted away the crates and buoys.

"This is it, Jeni!" Thomas shouted. "Big breath now, Jen! Big—"

A sound like metal pulling apart metal ripped through the cabin. The boat split in two. Water rushed in from all sides. The last thing Thomas saw was the blur of Jeni's terrified face reaching out for him before she was sucked backwards in a stream of bubbles.

❧

Vague shapes floated past him—pieces of wood he batted away as he swam frantically toward the surface. Powering through the wreckage, coming straight for him, he saw it:

A blurry gray hammerhead cutting through the water.

He screamed a stream of silent bubbles and tried to swim backwards. He looked back. The face of the hammerhead shark was right up next to him. He closed his eyes, already feeling the first gnash of the oncoming attack. But right before he was certain the shark was going to barrel into him, out of nowhere he felt two strong arms grip him around the waist, pulling him up into a stream of bubbles. When at last he breached the topside world, sputtering and hacking, in the surf next to him bobbed a man, a metal hammerhead shark helmet tipped up over his forehead like a catcher's helmet.

"You hold? *Da*?" the man said in a thick Russian accent, handing Thomas a buoy to cling to. Before Thomas could say a word, the man tipped the hammerhead helmet back down over his face and plunged back into the surf, returning a few moments later with Jeni in his arms.

A few red and white life rings bobbed past their heads. Jeni grabbed hold of one ring and clung to it for dear life, spitting out the last gulps of seawater from her lungs. Thomas reached into his pocket. Miracle of all miracles, his glasses were still there. He fit the wet glasses on his nose and wiped the lenses. Jeni's face came clear again, bobbing next to him. Before he could ask her if she was okay, a voice like a loudspeaker boomed above them, "Ahoy, comrades! Let's get you out of this mess!"

Thomas and Jeni both went a shade paler than they already were.

Out of the gloom a giant half-submerged submarine materialized, salt water streaming down its massive copper hull like some great mechanical whale. Standing by an open hatch on the main deck stood a stout figure, his head silhouetted by a giant spotlight that shone like a giant eye above him.

"Come on up!" the figure called again in his booming voice. "The Sieve are gone, I assure you! And if they're not, Boris the Hammerhead will surely track them down! Come on up!"

Jeni looked at Thomas. *Had they any other choice?* Not if they didn't want to die of hypothermia.

As usual, Jeni led the way. Holding on to the life ring, she swam toward the side of the giant submersible, Thomas swimming after her. Iron footholds protruded like staples from the side of the submarine. Jeni was the first up, and as she took the hand that extended out to her to pull her safely onto the deck, she gasped.

The man who had offered the helping hand had a familiar square jaw and a thick blond beard—it was Richie Mulvaney! He appeared almost identical to Crowley's impersonation, save for a deep red scar that stretched across one cheek, half-hidden by the thick curls of his beard.

As Thomas reached for the first foothold, the man in the hammerhead mask swam up next to him.

"You take? *Da?*" the man urged, passing Thomas something dark and dripping with seawater…his backpack!

"How did you…?" Thomas stammered.

The man chuckled, a hearty bellowing that rumbled up from his lungs. He spat a stream of water between the gap of his two front teeth before disappearing underwater once more.

Thomas clambered up the rungs and emerged, dripping, on the top deck of the submarine.

"Thomas," said Jeni, throwing her arms around him. "There's someone I want you to meet."

"It's Richie," said Jeni, grinning happily. "The *real* Richie."

"Hello, Thomas Creeper," said Richie Mulvaney, extending a massive hand out to Thomas to shake. Thomas took the hand apprehensively, gazing up at a face he had last seen crumbling away only to reveal the Sieve leader Crowley lurking beneath.

"I can tell by that dark look you have quite a story to share," said Richie. "There will be time enough for all explanations tonight. Welcome aboard the *Conch Whistle*, Thomas Creeper, the mighty seafaring home of Mulvaney's Raiders!"

BOOK
THREE:
Halls of Light,
Halls of Death

KEEP
OUT

X

Custodians and Preservers

Once inside the *Conch Whistle* Thomas and Jeni found themselves staring at a central chamber where various tubes hummed and wheezed above their heads like a living mechanical heart.

"This is our Viewing Deck," Richie proclaimed with a sweep of his arm.

A massive captain's chair sat in the center of the chamber like a throne, surrounded by an orchestra of levers and switches, as well as a network of more brass tubes that popped, hummed, and fizzled in sporadic concert. A large flat-paneled computer screen depicted various views of the ship: the deck where they had just descended; the port and starboard sides of the submersible; and one window, en larged more than the others, of a large jetty rising out of the mist. Set in either wall of the chamber—and, indeed, the floor itself beneath the captain's chair—were large glass panels that stretched like windows in a skyscraper, revealing the hidden depths illuminated by the *Conch Whistle*'s underwater lights. As Thomas and Jeni stood, soaked and stunned, on a gallery platform that ringed the center of the Viewing Deck like a circular track, they had the sensation that they were standing in a giant mobile aquarium. In front of their feet a wrought-iron spiral staircase descended to a larger central chamber below.

"Now the two of you, stay right where you are," said Richie. "Don't move."

Richie gave a swift tug on a large brass lever over his head. A dry blast of air like a warm wind tunnel shot down from two giant tubes over Thomas and Jeni's heads. Thomas and Jeni looked shocked and covered their faces at first until they realized what was happening: the dry blast dried their hair and clothes! Richie gave two swift tugs to another brass lever and two towels dropped down from a hidden chute. Still stunned, but no longer soaked, the two children took the towels gratefully while Richie made a sharp whistle with his thumb and pinkie. Out from a blast of steam a robot rolled up out of the shadows and stopped before Thomas and Jeni.

The robot had a cylindrical body like a hot water heater that sat atop a gleaming brass wheel not unlike the wheel on a unicycle. A small panel opened in its front, revealing what looked like a tiny elevator with a red button beside it.

"Go on!" said Richie, chuckling. "Press the button!"

There was a momentary whir and whiz, and then the elevator doors opened to reveal a steaming cup of tea.

Thomas handed the tea cup to Jeni who took it gratefully. The elevator doors closed. The robot let out a gurgle of steam, and a second cup appeared. Eyes wide with wonder, Thomas wrapped his fingers around the warm tea cup. He tipped back the cup, taking a long, deep sip, enjoying every drop of warmth from the tea and the sweet cinnamon smell that wafted up into his nose. *It was all too unbelievable for words!* he thought. The robot, having now completed its task, rolled back into the shadowed recesses of the chamber.

"I'm sorry for arriving so late," said Richie, descending the spiral staircase to the deck below. Thomas and Jeni followed the *Conch Whistle*'s captain down, holding on carefully to the copper railing. "We'd been scanning the land for days," Richie continued. "But we didn't think the Sieve would make their play so soon. We sighted the old fishing boat trolling the marshes and we came as quickly as we could."

Thomas and Jeni followed Richie down the spiral staircase until they reached the main chamber below.

"What happened?" Jeni asked. "Did you sink the boat?"

"Yes," Richie replied, looking pleased. "Boris came up

with the ramming idea. He has quite a hard head, especially when Otto's Aqua Socks are on full blast...."

Thomas raised an eyebrow and looked at Jeni. But Richie, crossing the grated floor and reaching the captain's chair, pressed a large button.

"Not a delicate approach, I'd say. No, not even safe," mused Richie. "But it did scare them off, didn't it? Now let me introduce you to my fantastic crew...ALL HANDS ON DECK!"

Richie let go of the button. A rippling arpeggio, like the sound of a massive trumpet, echoed through the hull of the *Conch Whistle*. Jeni grabbed hold of Thomas's hand, her face as excited as a game show contestant when the host is about to reveal what's behind the big prize door.

"Now, you've already met Boris, the speed-swimming champion of Ukraine," said Richie, pointing to the large panel on the starboard side of the Viewing Deck. In the green water illuminated by the submersible's lights swam the man in the hammerhead helmet who had saved Thomas and Jeni from drowning. He wore mesh socks on his feet with steel propellers attached to the heels. He took off across the bow at unbelievable speed, the propellers accelerating him through water as bubbles streamed from the corners of his helmet.

"The shark helmet connects to a breathing tank in his suit that provides additional air," Richie explained. "As for the famed Aqua Socks, well, you both have experienced first-hand their ramming speed!" Richie's scarred face beamed with pride. "It's only fitting that we introduce the creator of such an extraordinary invention, indeed, the genius behind the *Conch Whistle* herself. An Edison of the high seas! A Tesla of the emerald deep! I present to you, Otto the Second!"

A swiveling platform lowered from the ceiling in a blast of steam. With a smooth sliding motion, the platform descended to the floor of the Viewing Deck and a figure stepped off.

A grizzled old man with a drooping white moustache

materialized out of the steam. He wore thick black goggles with a number of optical lenses, much like a diamond jeweler might wear when examining the most minute detail in a precious diamond. His right arm was composed of intricately moving metal parts that whirred and clicked and seemed composed, like the ship, of an array of levers, gears, and tubes. Instead of a hand, he possessed a large brass Swiss Army knife, complete with wrenches, screwdrivers, chisels, hammers, and blades of all kinds, and something that looked as if it could properly juice a lemon. From the back elbow of this mechanical arm a long tube protruded, curling upward to attach to a brass canister slung across the old man's back that seemed to hum with pressure like the pneumatic wheeze of a large air compressor (*pneumatic*, being a fancy word for something that operates by air or contains gas under pressure, not unlike your little brother or sister after too many tacos!).

"*Willkommen, kinder!*" bellowed Otto in a voice deep and resonant as a German tuba. "Our captain is quite prone to hyperbole, but his praise is not entirely unfounded! The *Conch Whistle* is my dream of copper and steam! She can reach seventy knots in under ten point four three seconds, and can cover three hundred nautical miles without restoring its steam reactor. It is my principal aim to make her ready for the Aquatic Steam Relays in Ystad next summer!"

"And indeed, you shall, old friend," said Richie, reaching out and patting the side of the pneumatic cannister on the old man's back, inadvertently loosening a gauge that began to spit a steady stream of steam.

The old man grumbled something in German while Richie leapt to tighten the gauge, frowning and apologizing profusely, which seemed to make the scar on his cheek glow a brighter red. Jeni giggled helplessly at the sight. Once order had been restored, the old German engineer clicked his tall boots, made a sharp nod of his head, shook his drooping moustache, and climbed back onto the platform. He uttered a loud, "*Oben!*" and the platform began to ascend back to the chamber above.

"Next, may I present Boris's bride and sweetheart, Kasha Annikova!" continued Richie, with a dramatic flourish. "Known from Prague to Piccadilly Circus for her death-defying knife-throwing and impossible contortions that would make a caterpillar envious! Ladies and gentlemen, I give you...THE SIBERIAN DAGGER!"

Out from the shadows of the upper deck, a lithe figure back-flipped across the ledge, then somersaulted through the hissing air, landing next to Richie, hands on her hips. Thomas's mouth dropped open. Kasha was the most beautiful woman he had ever seen, with raven-dark hair, high cheekbones, and fire-truck-red lips. Electric blue eyeshadow coated the lids of her bright, almond-shaped eyes, giving the knife-wielding contortionist an even wilder and more exotic expression. She wore a black-and-white-striped swimsuit, with a sash filled with dozens of different daggers draped across her chest. The handles of the blades were crusted with glittering jewels, which cast a kaleidoscope of color and light across her face. Her expression was one of playful defiance, as if she were just waiting for someone to dare her to do the impossible.

"There's one more of us you need to meet," said Richie. "I can't say there's anyone, or rather *anything*, quite like him in the world. Mouth? Are you here with us?"

The captain's chair swiveled around. At only four feet tall, the figure who had been sitting there all along, hidden by the swooping back of the chair, now appeared to Thomas and Jeni in all his confounding abnormality.

"He won't speak to anyone but me, I'm afraid," said Richie. "I found him living alone in the Maldives with nothing but an old suitcase. The return address on the case indicated some place in the English Cotswolds. We think he came into contact with a very rare tropical disease while marooned on the island. He has a very curious talent. Will you show our new friends, Mouth?"

As wide as he was tall, Mouth rose from his chair and waddled forward into a bright circle of light. His skin was a mottled yellowish-green with purple spots that bloomed up under the shadows of his enormous chin. He wore a baggy, sweat-stained linen shirt and matching linen shorts. *He looks like a frog and a man mutated together*, Thomas thought as he took in the sheer scientific miracle—or curse—of the creature known as Mouth.

"Mouth has the most remarkable tongue," Richie continued. "Eight feet long, it can shoot out and seize just about any object, animate or inanimate. Then, once he has properly consumed the object, he can understand everything about the object's history and provenance—where the item had been made, who had owned it, all the various places it had been. He's quite good at detecting imitation crab in California rolls, I might add."

Mouth glanced at Thomas. Thomas cringed and closed his eyes. A second later he heard something whip through the air as something was whisked off his shoulders. When he opened his eyes again his suspicions were confirmed: *the towel around his neck was gone*...or at least most of it.

A white corner still hung out the side of Mouth's green lips but it disappeared with a loud slurp a second later. Letting out a generous belch, Mouth waddled over and whispered in Richie's ear.

Richie smiled and nodded a few times. "He says: the towel was made of 100 percent cotton by Trifold Industries in London, shipped by a diesel-fueled cargo ship to Connecticut, where it was sold by Walmart...and that Otto needs to go easy on the bleach."

"That's incredible!" said Jeni. "He must have the most amazing digestive system!"

Richie's smile collapsed to an unmistakable wince. "Let's just say he has his own private bathroom. Now, if we are all sufficiently well acquainted and you are both recovered from your frightening episode under water, it's high time I told you why we're here." He clicked a button on the arm of the captain's chair and a new image appeared on the flat screen. It appeared to be a sketched diagram of the skeletal structure of a creature with long sections of ringed vertebrae.

"We were on the hunt for a new species of poisonous sea snake," said Richie over his shoulder, "whose blood is rumored to cure blindness. We were in the Barrier Reef off the coast of Australia when we received a video distress call from my uncle, Pop."

Richie hit another button and the worried face of Pop Mulvaney appeared on the screen.

"Richie," the priest whispered, "I found the Weapon! I knew it was still somewhere in Gloomsbury! I should have known Sneed couldn't have gone far in his attempt to bury it. Please come as fast as you can. I fear that my time is running out..."

Richie hit stop on the video, his expression crestfallen.

"Pop was found dead the next day," said Richie grimly. He hit another button and the sketch of a terrifyingly familiar face appeared, wearing a black bowler hat and wire-rimmed spectacles.

"Crowley!" said Thomas.

"Aye," said Richie. "Pop had been tracking Crowley and the Sieve for years. It's the reason why he would never accept my offer to leave his post. You see, he stayed in Gloomsbury to unravel the dark mystery of its past, what he called the great Gloomsbury Secret. I understand that their leader, that grinning devil Crowley, found a picture of me in Pop's house and pretended to be me, tricking you two into divulging what you had learned. It seems he stumbled across an older photograph of me, before this little encounter." Richie pointed to the deep red scar on his cheek. "But that's a story for another time. Now we must continue my uncle's dream of so many years: to stop the Sieve from spreading their misery any further."

Kasha twirled a glittering dagger in the palm of her hand.

"We find them and it will be slice and dice time, Captain!" she snarled.

Mouth belched in enthusiastic agreement.

"Indeed, my friends, their time will come. But we must be careful. Crowley's magic is old and strong," Richie acknowledged. "However, we did manage to gather some useful intelligence before sinking his boat. The Sieve gathered together on the deck, twenty of them at least, and traveled like a swarm through the fog. I suspect that however powerful Crowley may be, that kind of grand display must drain him somehow, which may mean there is a window of vulnerability as he seeks to regenerate his powers. We've located the longitude and latitude coordinates referenced in Pop's diary. You two budding detectives found those, did you not?"

Thomas and Jeni nodded their heads.

"Yes," Thomas chimed in. "But we didn't know if they meant south or north or east or west."

"Ah, of course," Richie agreed, brandishing his pipe from a side pocket. "Pop sent me the same coordinates, in an encoded file with the video message you just saw. Which brought us here to this location, to where Our Lady of the Waves resides."

"Our Lady of the Waves?" Jeni asked, perplexed.

"You shall see soon enough, my young friend," Richie replied, removing a match from his shirt pocket and flicking it against the side of his captain's chair. Lowering the match into the bowl of his pipe, he took a few puffs. Sweet-smelling tobacco smoke filled the chamber, not unlike the smell of the calming tea that Thomas and Jeni had drained to the very last drop.

"Boris is bringing up the on-the-spot feed right now," said Richie as he settled into the captain's chair. "Let's see what all the hubbub is about."

Richie tapped on the keyboard, and Boris's hammerhead helmet appeared on the screen. Boris waved and the camera view switched from the *Conch Whistle* cameras to one fastened to Boris's hammerhead helmet. The camera lurched one way, then another, the view obscured by a steady stream of bubbles. Kasha cursed in Russian as Boris's thick fingers appeared in front of the lens, tightening the camera brackets.

Boris descended and Richie directed the *Conch Whistle*'s lights to illuminate his path. Out of the darkness a large jetty appeared, covered in barnacles and seaweed.

"There she is!" exclaimed Richie, as Boris swam down to the base of the jetty. "Our Lady of the Waves!"

A statue appeared out of the murky water. Boris moved closer, the camera mounted to his hammerhead helmet bringing the murky image into clearer view. Thomas and Jeni gathered around the viewing screen to better make out the details of the strange and unexpected apparition. Materializing on the screen in front of them they could see the statue of a woman on the bottom of the sea floor. She was dressed in flowing Grecian robes, her shoulders draped with green and black seaweed like tentacles. Her arms were outstretched, as if reaching out for something or someone, her cupped palms filled with a slimy offering of seaweed. Small spider crabs crawled up and down her arms and legs, skittering away from the underwater flashlight that now appeared in Boris's massive hand. Slowly, carefully, he brushed aside the tangle of seaweed in the statue's hands. Jeni grabbed Thomas's shoulder and held her breath. Within the cup of the statue's outstretched hands a small, narrow box sat, speckled with green algae. The lid of the box was open. Boris moved the beam of the flashlight and peered inside.

But the box was empty.

❧

In the small mess hall in the bowels of the submersible, Mouth—who also doubled as ship's cook—brought Thomas and Jeni a plate of fried fish wrapped in seaweed, apparently a daily ration aboard the *Conch Whistle*.

Thomas was hesitant at first. After all, Mouth's taste in

food ran the gamut from old towels to whatever his tongue could lash out of the air, according to Richie. Thomas took a hesitant bite. To his pleasant surprise, he discovered that the fish was delicious—crunchy, perfectly balanced between salty and sweet. Mouth made a small bow before retreating back into the shadows, where he finished the remainder of the meal, smacking his lips and burping loudly.

"So, dead end, huh?" said Jeni between bites of Mouth's tasty cooking. "Did you think there was really going to be something down there?"

"I don't know," said Thomas glumly, shrugging his shoulders. "I keep thinking about what the glasses showed me, seeing Elijah Creeper the First and Sneed on the beach below Dyre Dunes. They were loading something heavy onto the boat."

"The statue, right?" said Jeni thinking quickly. "But that's gotta weigh, what? A *bajillion* pounds?"

"Right," said Thomas, sighing. "I think that Elijah Creeper the First and Sneed found this weapon, something that could really hurt the Sieve, and they buried it with the statue because they knew the statue would protect it somehow. I think they knew they were going to die and this was their last-ditch effort to hide the weapon from the Sieve."

Jeni frowned and nodded her head. "Well, that's certainly one theory, professor. But there's something else we should be worried about."

"What's that?" asked Thomas. "What could be more worrying than an all-powerful Sieve monster wanting to turn Gloomsbury into worm-filled zombies?"

"Your father," Jeni replied wryly. "Our parents have no idea where either of us are. They've probably already gone to the police! Did you tell your mom or dad about any of this, Thomas? Pop's murder? The Sieve? The magic glasses?"

"Well, no..." Thomas began. The events of the past few hours were so out-of-this-world, so utterly insane, that he hadn't really had time to think about the reality that waited for him back on land, let alone catch his breath. He could just see his father's irate face. Maybe if it was the end, if they couldn't find the Weapon, then Crowley and the Sieve would be invincible. Richie could at least bring the *Conch Whistle* to the surface of Gloomsbury Bay so he could see his father faint before he launched into the world's worst lecture from Creeper Family Protocol. Rule #37, a new addition: *A mortician in training has no business mixing with seafaring weirdos whose favorite pastime was asking underwater sculpture for magical artifacts....*

"Greetings, *kinder*. Might I join you?" a deep voice bellowed from the door of the mess hall, interrupting their conversation.

The human-mechanical form of Otto the Second swivelled through the doorway and seated himself atop a large mobile stool with various wheels and adjustable platforms. "This is yours, I believe?" he asked, holding aloft Thomas's backpack, which he had left on the upper Viewing Deck. "You must excuse me," said Otto. "I am, how you say, a bad dropper of eaves." A withered smile stretched between the ends of the old man's swooping white moustache. "Might these be the magic wire-rimmed spectacles you are referring to? I found them in your bag while drying out your belongings. I also found your curious pocket watch, Herr Thomas, which I'm afraid to report is quite waterlogged." The old engineer withdrew the Aldous pocket watch from the damp backpack. Thomas could see, to his great disappointment, water sloshing the minute and second hands in crazy directions.

"But do not worry! I shall bring it to my Den of Oddities, where I am quite confident that with a little tinkering, *ja*, I shall restore it to working condition!" He handed the backpack over to Thomas. "But I would also like to examine these magical spectacles, if you would permit me?"

"Of course," Thomas replied, taking the enchanted spectacles out of the backpack pocket. Touching the lenses, just for a moment, he could feel their strange magnetism surging through his fingertips like an electric pulse. Quickly, he handed the spectacles over to Otto, who held them gingerly between thick tweezers that extended from his mechanical hand. The old engineer clicked a button on the side of his goggles and a small tube with a small glowing bulb on its end (much like a reading light) extended from one side. Otto peered at the spectacles, switching rapidly between his many optical lenses, scrutinizing every detail of the mysterious glasses.

"Curious…very curious indeed," Otto murmured. "These are not made of glass. Yes, everything about their *appearance* would suggest so. But they are manufactured of a foreign substance. An alien substance, in fact."

"Alien?" said Thomas.

"*Jawhol, mein Freund!*" said Otto. "They are not unique, however. Come, I will show you!"

Otto swiveled away from the table, gesturing for Thomas and Jeni to accompany him. They followed Otto's bobbing compressor pack through a darkened corridor in the belly of the great submersible, a multitude of tubes humming and wheezing above their heads as they passed. The corridor widened, opening into a chamber about the size of a single-car garage.

❧

In the center of the chamber, positioned directly beneath a large spotlight, sat a massive work table covered with all manner of curious odds and ends: massive brass diving helmets with black rubber breathing tubes; a half-built diving sphere, shaped like the shell of a turtle; various spear-like rods with glass-bulb chambers flashing intermittently with zaps of electricity. It was a chaotic scene, full of loose nuts and bolts, piles of tangled copper wires, and piles of white rags blackened with grease. The walls were covered with nautical maps, diagrams, and machine schematics. Below the maps, at eye level, a long ring of rubber compartments encircled the chamber, stickers on their tiny glass doors detailing the specific parts stored within.

Suddenly, the room listed to one side, and a dull groan sounded through the chambers of the submersible.

"Don't worry, *mein kinder*, it is just the deep channel currents," Otto said with a chuckle as he glided across the tilting floor on his stool. "They can get a bit turbulent this time of year." The submersible righted itself, and Otto removed a small black suitcase from under the table and set it on a small work bench in front of Thomas and Jeni. He hit the button on the side of his goggles, and the dangling head lamp glowed with a brighter intensity.

"I collect the oddities of this world," Otto said, smiling impishly beneath his white whiskers, "and perhaps some from a few other worlds as well. When you find an object on a beach, are you not curious about its creator? This is the great philosophical dilemma of the Watchmaker's Universe. Have either of you heard that one?"

"Yes," said Jeni, piping up. "If you find a watch then you assume there must be a watchmaker."

"Indeed! *Gut gemacht, Frauleine!*" exclaimed Otto. "The captain was right when he said we were dealing with two top-notch students!"

Holding out his mechanical arm, Otto's metal fingers retracted to reveal an array of smaller chisel-like tools with jagged edges. He inserted one into a large brass lock on the suitcase and turned it ninety degrees clockwise; the lock clicked open.

"These enchanted spectacles are called by many names," continued Otto. "Some know them as the 'Eyes of Time.' For me, an avid collector of such mysteries over the years, I just call them by one word..." His grizzled face darkened. "Trouble."

The lid opened, and Thomas's jaw nearly dropped to the greasy floor. Resting within a series of intricately cut blue velvet holes were spectacles of all shapes and sizes—glasses with round lenses, others with a single, monocle-type lens. The glasses came in a variety of frames, too: one was bone-colored, another one painted a brilliant turquoise; there was even one that looked as if it had been made for a robot, with loose circuitry wires hanging from square-shaped lenses. Thomas was just about to ask Otto about that pair when the old engineer held out Thomas's enchanted wire-rimmed spectacles and tucked them into a snug carved-out space where they fit like the right key into the right lock. "There you go," he whispered.

"Mulvaney's Raiders are the custodians of such wondrous things," said Otto in a solemn voice. "While I dislike the term *raider*, we do steal when we must. But we also preserve, hoping to protect the world from those who would use such wonders for evil. We don't know who fashioned these glasses, or how many exist in the world, but we do know that they are made of a material found nowhere else on this planet."

"So Crowley found two of them?" Jeni asked. "I mean, we have Pop's pair—"

"And Crowley has another," Thomas confirmed. "In my dream…I mean, it was like a waking dream…Crowley kept asking me where I got my spectacles from. He must want them back. Maybe the ones I found in Pop's cellar can do things his pair can't? I don't know."

"What *is* clear," said Otto, closing the suitcase, "is that we must safeguard them to prevent Crowley from using them to cause more mischief. Would you mind, Thomas, if I kept your pair here, for safekeeping?"

Thomas nodded, relieved to be rid of them. Sure, the feeling of moving through time was wonderful…but terrifying. He would be perfectly fine if he never went through that wretched wormhole of mist ever again.

"But," said Otto, smiling and waving a grease-stained finger in the air, "perhaps I may offer you something in return? A trade, perhaps?"

The old engineer swiveled away and rolled over to a locker set into the wall. Otto opened the door and cursed as a river of mechanical parts poured onto the floor. As Otto sifted through the heap of objects, a metal bird with mechanical wings and red electric eyes flew out of the pile, grazing past Thomas's ear. The bird circled over his shoulders a few times, to Thomas and Jeni's delight, before coming to rest on a hissing metal pipe above their heads.

"Here they are!" exclaimed Otto. "The great Knutson Ocular-Occult Goggles! The Ocu-Occu!"

At first glance, the goggles in Otto's hand resembled nothing more than old-fashioned aviator's goggles or perhaps something a skier might have donned at the turn of the century. The frames gleamed like black obsidian, and the teardrop-shaped lenses looked like the face of an owl. An eerie glow lit up the glass lenses, as if they had been manufactured of exotic green amethyst or chiseled from somewhere deep in the walls of a glacial ice cave. A triangular beak between the lenses hooked into a broad leather strap that fixed the goggles to the wearer's head.

"*Atem des Geistes,*" whispered Otto reverently as he showed them the inscription burned into the leather strap. "*Breath of the ghost.* These belonged to Heinrich Knutson, my predecessor and self-proclaimed biologist of the dead. It is believed that on October 15, 1947, he captured the breath of a ghost upon two trays of glass."

Otto's mechanical hand delicately handed the Knutson Ocular-Occult Goggles to Thomas, who took them with some trepidation, feeling the same combination of fear and fascination that he had felt handling the Sieve's enchanted spectacles.

"I realize now," said Otto, his eyes twinkling beneath the thick glass of his own goggles, "that we failed to find what we came for today because the weapon was never intended to be seen with ordinary eyes. I have since pulled up Heinrich's notes. He was quite meticulous, you can imagine, on any topic concerning the deceased. He believed that in order to see something unnatural, you had to see *through* unnatural eyes. The eyes of a ghost! So, come, *kinder*! Let us see if the great Lady is down there, and whether she will come to our aid in this fateful hour and help turn the tide against this menace once and for all!"

XI

The Lady, the Weapon

Thomas had agreed to the plan, but it felt like agreeing to skydive for the first time. He felt brave and uncertain all at once. It was a horrible mixed-up feeling that set his heart racing and his palms glistening with sweat. At a large circular door in the floor in the *Conch Whistle*'s submerging bay, Otto handed Thomas a small brass mouthpiece shaped like an old radio microphone.

"This micro-respirator fits snugly between your teeth," Otto explained. "It will give you at least five minutes of oxygen. I wish we had proper diving gear for you, Thomas, but we took on a boarder a few months back who cleaned us out. Lesson learned, I'm afraid. Never board a magician with horrible debt."

"It's fine," said Thomas, inserting the device between his teeth. The air felt cold and metallic in his throat, but he soon became accustomed to the rhythmic whoosh of his breath in his ears.

"Boris will also have a weight belt with a buoyancy compensator," Otto continued. "Very easy to operate. The button on the top of the belt increases buoyancy, the button on the bottom decreases it. *Ja*?"

Thomas nodded.

"Please be careful, Thomas," said Jeni, appearing next to him.

"Frgghmrrgana!" said Thomas. Jeni shrugged, and Thomas removed his mouthpiece. "I said don't worry," said Thomas. "The Ocular-Occult Goggles will let me know if there's a ghost down there. I know, I know. You don't believe in ghosts, but not so long ago, we didn't believe in the Sieve either."

Jeni opened her mouth to say something biting as a comeback, but Boris appeared at Thomas's shoulder, standing over the boy like a mountain of muscle.

"Time to swim, *Tomac*," said Boris.

A shrill bell rang through the small chamber. Thomas glanced nervously at Jeni. He knew he couldn't hide anything from her.

The door in the floor opened to reveal a round tank about the size of an elevator.

"Once we are inside metal can, door to submerging bay will close," Boris explained as he climbed into the tank. "Richie hit button and ocean opens. *Da?* Come, *Tomac*!" Boris waved to Thomas. "Timing is now!"

"Thom—" Jeni began.

"Don't worry," said Thomas, trying to appear confident and brave. "I-I'll be right back."

Before Jeni could say another word, he climbed down into the tank next to Boris, who had already fastened on his hammerhead helmet. Thomas inserted the micro-respirator between his teeth, and the circular air-lock door above their heads started to close. Jeni's face appeared in the glass window of the air-lock door. Thomas gave her his best impression of the wave of a warrior heading off to battle…but it was a flimsy attempt. *I should have said something cooler than 'Don't worry! I'll be right back!'* he thought. Cliff Henderson, the actor who played Ken Darby in all the spy movies he loved, would have kissed the girl before leaping from a burning building or into a pit of deadly vipers. If only he could find a way to tell Jeni what he was feeling without the cursed Creeper-ness spoiling everything. *I solved your cipher*, he wanted to tell her. *I like you too. More than a friend. And I don't care if that messes everything up. I think it's worth the risk.*

Boris strapped a weight belt around Thomas's waist and tightened the clasp until it was a snug fit. Thomas felt an immediate tug of gravity, as if he'd singlehandedly consumed one hundred of Sal's Steak 'n' Cheese Double Stuffers all by himself. He fit the straps of the Ocu-Occu Goggles tight over his ears and watched, amazed, as the world began to morph before his eyes.

Everything in the tank—the iron walls, Boris's strange hammerhead helmet, the air-lock door above—turned an eerie shade of green. *Otto never said anything about the world turning green*, he thought. But he didn't have long to ponder the weird change in vision. The exterior submersible door slid open. Cold water surged into the tank. Thomas breathed in deeply through his micro-respirator as he felt his body start to sink. The change in pressure clicked in his ears as he descended through the hull and into the dark ocean depths. Staring up at the *Conch Whistle*'s copper belly, he could see Richie, Otto, Kasha, and Jeni in the Viewing Deck looking down at him. Jeni waved and Thomas gave her a Ken Darby thumbs-up.

❧

As Thomas continued to sink, the water around him (cast in shades of eerie green, thanks to the Ocu-Occu Goggles) swarmed with ghostly forms of dead fish and sea life. It was like a phantom highway, Thomas thought, riveted by the sight. That is, until the ghost-fish swam *through* him, giving him the same icy chill as he had felt whenever Silvie passed through him. Below, Thomas could make out the sandy bottom of the ocean floor and the shadow of some massive creature. If he could have screamed without dropping the micro-respirator he would have at that moment. *It was the ghost of a prehistoric sea monster with a long, rotting tail!* Thomas realized, his heart pounding in his chest. The ghost-monster slipped behind the back side of the jetty and disappeared in a flurry of sand and silt. Noticing Thomas's alarm but unable to detect its cause, Boris flashed Thomas another thumbs-up. Thomas gave Boris a shaky wave and returned the thumbs-up. For a moment, he wished he could yank the Ocu-Occu Goggles off his head and be done with the undead ocean world—the *live* ocean world, with great white sharks and spiny thornfish, was bad enough.

The *Conch Whistle*'s underwater spotlights appeared over Thomas's shoulder and settled on the sandy floor, illuminating timber pilings and a few crabs peeking out of their barnacled holes. Boris swam down into the murk, the whirling propellers of his Aqua Socks casting a steady stream of bubbles in his wake. Thomas followed, kicking as hard as he could to keep up. Soon he and Boris were hovering right next to the outstretched arms of the statue of Our Lady of the Waves.

The propellers on Boris's Aqua Socks stilled. With a massive hand he pointed to one of two buttons on Thomas's weight belt. Thomas understood and nodded. He pressed the button to feel the upper portion of the belt inflate, allowing him to hover just above the sandy bottom. It was then, peering through the Ocu-Occu Goggles, that he saw the pale hand, lit by a dazzling green light, wave him closer. Out of the chiseled limbs of the statue a beautiful ghost-woman suddenly appeared.

For a moment Thomas forgot to breathe as the ghost reached out her hands. Like the statue, she wore a flowing dress belted high at the waist and pinned at the shoulders with starfish. She reached out a pale hand to stroke his cheek, and he felt a strange cooling sensation, much like an ice cube sliding across his skin. Within Thomas's mind he heard the gentle rush of waves, and in between the gentle whoosh-whoosh, he could make out the ghost-woman's soft words.

Why do you seek it, Thomas Creeper? How can I be certain that you will not be corrupted by its power until you are no different from the monsters you seek to vanquish?

Thomas focused his thoughts on his reply. *I don't want power!* he thought urgently. *I want this all to be over! I want my life back to normal!*

The ghost-woman smiled.

You will never be normal, Thomas Creeper. But, so be it! You have dug this far. You must only dig a little deeper....

The ghost-woman gestured toward the statue's feet. Thomas pressed the button on his weight belt to release the air in a stream of bubbles, and as he did so he dropped to the ocean floor, landing on his knees in a cloud of silt. Clearing away the seaweed and rocks at the foot of the statue, he began to dig. He dug for some time, silt and mud billowing up around his goggles until it was hard to see much of anything.

Feeling something hard at the bottom of the hole, Thomas paused, allowing the silt and mud to settle. Peering inside the hole, he blinked in disbelief. A small brass plug—just like the kind you'd find in an old claw-foot bathtub—rested at the bottom of the hole, a rusted metal chain coiled beside it. Thomas glanced up but the shimmering ghost had disappeared, leaving only a faint trail of phosphorescence behind her. Boris descended to the ocean floor and grinned at Thomas through the glass panel of his hammerhead helmet. Thomas took a deep breath through his micro-respirator, closed his fingers around the chain, and pulled.

A cloud of fine sand billowed upward, as if driven upward by some hidden current. Thomas closed his eyes, feeling sand grains rip through his hair and suit. When the water cleared again, he could see that a narrow tunnel had opened beneath him. Wedged to the right of the tunnel, he could see the pale stone of the statue's hair and crown coming out of the shadows. She had sunk some ten feet into the soft silt. Boris removed a waterproof flare from his belt, snapped it on, and dropped it down the hole. There was no way Boris could fit down that hole with his blocky, muscular body. The rest was up to Thomas.

The air in his micro-respirator was becoming harder to draw. Thomas knew he didn't have much air, or much time. He hit the upper button on his belt to increase the weight and help him sink into the hole. The sand walls felt as if they were pressing in on him as he descended, and the green light of the flare below lit his feet in a neon glow. Thomas closed his eyes, feeling claustrophobic, reminding him of the time the coffin lid had snapped shut with him inside as he was trying to reach a dust bunny with a Dustbuster. Then, just when he felt he couldn't stand it any longer, Thomas spied the box—another box, just like the empty one that had rested in the statue's hands. This one lay on a stone that extended out into the tunnel like a little shelf, just below Thomas's feet. The box in the statue's hand had been a decoy! he suddenly realized. Pressing the upper button on his belt again, Thomas dropped faster, deeper into the hole. Just as the air in the micro-respirator was becoming thin and hard to draw into his lungs, Thomas finally reached the shelf. He seized the box, stuffing it between his belt and his wet suit. Then he hit the lower Inflate button as hard as he could. Then he hit it again, only to see a flurry of white powder whoosh out of the side of the belt. He continued to sink down into the dark hole. The flare beneath his feet sizzled out, and everything went dark.

The respirator sputtered. Thomas kicked hard, trying to make his way back up the tunnel as the respirator finally went dry. Flailing, his heart thumping in his ears, he careened into the side of the statue, knocking any breath out of him. The air in his lungs gave out. Salt water rushed into his lungs, his screams choked off in a stream of bubbles.

❧

"C'mon, Thomas! Please! You can't die! Please!"

Thomas opened his eyes as something scratched in his throat. A thin tube made a sucking sound, much like the trash compactor in the kitchen sink. Leaning over, Thomas yanked the tube from his mouth and retched violently, salty water emptying out of his lungs. The retracting tube scooted across the floor until it came to a sharp *clink!* inside Otto the Second's mechanical arm. Thomas sat up on the floor of the submerging bay, spitting out the last of the seawater. The Ocu-Occu Goggles lay on the floor beside him, and the world had regained its normal coloration, the eerie green and the ghostly figures gone.

"Welcome back, my friend!" Otto bellowed.

"I swear, Thomas!" cried Jeni waving her fist in front of him. "If you do something stupid like this again, I swear. . . ." Jeni trailed off, fuming.

"Not funny joke," said Boris standing over him, his hammerhead helmet under one arm.

"Boris shoved the statue out of the way and pulled you out," Otto told Thomas as he helped him to his feet.

"Th-thanks," Thomas stammered, as Richie wrapped a warm towel around his shoulders.

Thomas felt beneath his weighted belt and brought out a small box.

"And he kept a death grip on the treasure, to boot!" Richie exclaimed in wonder.

"Well, go ahead, *mein Freund*," said Otto smiling, as everyone jostled in for a closer look. "Go on! You might as well open it since you risked your life to bring it back to the ship!"

Thomas unlatched the rusted hinge on the wet box. He opened the lid to reveal three small glass vials, each one with its stopper still intact. One held a tightly rolled scroll of paper; the second, a copper ring with a blue gemstone; and the third, a dusting of white powder. Holding the first vial up to the light, they could see that the scroll was fastened by a miniature wax seal. Thomas opened the vial.

"Allow me," said Otto, breaking the seal with a quick turn of a small blade from his mechanical hand tool chest.

Thomas unrolled the note. Immediately, he recognized the flowing cursive script as that of his great-grandfather, Elijah Creeper the First.

"'I, Elijah Creeper,'" Thomas read aloud in a shaky voice, "'in concert with James Hieronymus Sneed, bury this time capsule beneath the waves to ensure the destruction of the Sieve. First, the ring…'" Thomas removed the stopper on the second vial. Carefully, he slipped out the small copper ring. "'Whoever wears this will be protected within a luminous shield of sapphire light, blinding even to the Sieve…" Thomas paused, remembering the chant from his ancestor in the vision gifted by the magic glasses beneath Dyre Dunes, how he told the Sieve that the blue fire would protect him. He must have found a way of preserving that power within the copper ring. "As for the miniature Narwhal tusk…'" Thomas picked up the third vial. "'…It has been recovered at great pains from a Scandinavian mystic. In a moment of crisis, the tusk shall expand to become a fearsome needle against dark forces. It is called the Narwhal Needle….'"

Thomas held the last vial up to the light. "The Narwhal Needle?" he said, bewildered. "But it's just a pile of dust…I swear I didn't break it…" He looked at the expectant gazes of his comrades with pleading eyes. "I'm pretty sure I hit the statue before I passed out. That couldn't have broken the Narwhal Needle, could it?"

"Thomas…" Jeni began, trying to comfort him. But Thomas wouldn't hear any of it. He ran from the chamber, down through a dark artery of the ship, until he came to the mess hall. He sank down at the table, his head in his hands. Tears blurred his eyes. He felt exhausted and ridiculous. He had risked everything only to smack headfirst into yet another dead end. How could they defeat the Sieve without the Narwhal Needle? The Sieve would go on forever, and all the good people who tried to stop them—like David and Pop—would die.

A hand landed on his shoulder, cool and calm. Jeni appeared next to him, wearing a wet suit, her strawberry-blonde hair tied into a ponytail, a pair of goggles propped up on her head.

"You never give up, professor," she said quietly, "and you can't now."

"It's over, Jeni," Thomas mumbled. "You saw it! The Narwhal Needle, the great Weapon, is freakin' dust," he scoffed. "It's all crap, Jeni. We can't do anything about it, and you're stupid if you think otherwise."

"Fine!" Jeni barked. "Then I'm stupid! Big old block of stupid! That's me! Everybody take a look at the big stupid loser who won't give up when her best friend is ready to throw in the towel like a total pansy!" she hollered.

"Who are you calling a pansy?" Thomas shouted furiously, leaping to his feet.

The air bristled between them, charged with angry energy. And then Jeni smiled. The smile widened. Thomas grinned ruefully in response. "I'm sorry for calling you stupid, Jen," he said, putting his arms around her shoulders. Thomas leaned his wet head against her own and squeezed her tight. "I know you don't believe in ghosts…But with the Ocu-Occu Goggles, I can see ghosts, Jen. And Our Lady of the Waves was there. I met her."

"Well then," said Jeni after a long thoughtful pause. "I guess you need to go ask her how to fix this mess, huh?" She handed him the Ocu-Occu Goggles, the owl-like lenses twinkling with faint green luminescence. I think your ghost lady might be our only shot at fixing the Narwhal Needle."

Thomas hated to admit it but once again Jeni Myers was right.

❧

This time Jeni wasn't going to risk any chance of losing her best friend, even if he tended to run off at the mouth and call her unpleasant names. She blamed it on the pressure of everything getting to him—the battle against Crowley and the Sieve, finding a broken Weapon, not to mention the *actual* underwater pressure of the ocean. She suited up and jumped into Boris's "metal can" next to Thomas. The door opened, and they began to sink side by side into the depths below.

Outside the air lock of the submerging bay, Jeni flashed

Thomas a thumbs-up sign and they swam down into the chilly water, pierced by the twin lights from the *Conch Whistle*. Thomas couldn't help but feel that he was tempting fate for the second time that day (third, if they counted almost dying in the wreck of the Sieve's ship). Floating through the green underwater world, ignoring the disconcerting chill of ghost-fish passing through him, they finally reached the ocean floor. Jeni followed Thomas to where the statue sat in the half-moon of the jetty. Thomas removed the small vial of powder from his pocket.

They waited. Thomas peered through the Ocu-Occu Goggles. He spotted a darting school of fish—live ones for a change—and a tangle of seaweed fluttering in the current, but no Lady of the Waves. Then, from the tunnel where Thomas had retrieved the box, a green shimmer grew, and Our Lady of the Waves materialized in Thomas's goggles as if being constructed from the ground up: first two feet and legs; then a swirl of her dress; then the hips, chest, shoulders; and finally her face. Then Thomas heard her silken voice whispering in his ears:

The true Weapon, Thomas, is what lies within you—inside the shield of your heart. The Needle can channel only what is already abundant and manifest within you. It is the pure goodness in the heart of whoever wields the Needle that powers its ability to repel evil. What is in your heart, Thomas Creeper?

Thomas seized Jeni's hand, raising it toward the ghost as if it were proof of some great truth: he cared.

I don't want to cause pain like the Sieve, he thought. *I don't want to rob the world of good people like David and Pop who made the world better each day by living in it. I want to help others whenever I can, whatever the cost to myself, maybe even help the dead if they'd give me some privacy.*

The Lady smiled and floated closer, wrapping her hands around Thomas and Jeni's clasped hands. Thomas shivered as he felt a cold rush through him.

Do you swear it, Thomas Creeper? Would you forfeit your life, if you were to veer to the path of evil? Thomas nodded. *So be it! Release the vial to me!*

Thomas handed her the vial. The Lady waved her fingers slightly until the stopper came loose and particles of white dust billowed forth from the vial. The particles formed a circle that began to spin, coalescing into a miniature whirlpool that grew larger and larger until Thomas feared it would drag them both inside its swirling vortex. Instead, the whirlpool began to radiate toward the surface, propelling Thomas and Jeni upward along with it. The whirlpool thrust them beyond the surface of the waves, hurling them like a wild roller coaster ride into the air. As they started to fall, screaming and spitting out their respirators, the whirlpool slowly descended, depositing them on the barnacled jetty. The last spume of water rippled down the barnacled rocks. As fast as it had appeared, the whirlpool was gone. Jeni and Thomas looked at each other as terror gave way to astonishment, astonishment to uncontrolled laughter. Neither of them had words to explain the marvelous progression of events that had taken them from the ocean floor to the top of the jetty. And they never would. Suddenly, there was a wild churning in the waves beside the jetty and the massive copper hull of the *Conch Whistle* made an emergency resurfacing. The hatch opened and Richie, Boris, Otto, and Kasha rushed topside, spotting Thomas and Jeni standing on the jetty, quite unharmed and still quite amused.

Thomas glanced down, realizing with astonishment that he held, tightly clenched in his right fist, a slender white dagger. The Narwhal Needle! And it was intact! As if responding to his touch, the bottom of the Needle adjusted, making small lined grooves to accommodate his thumb and fingers. *A handle carved for only his hand!* Thomas could hear the whispering voice of the Lady in his head:

So be it, Thomas Creeper! May Love and Good Fortune be your allies tonight and all the dark nights that lie ahead of you!

"I...told...you," Jeni said, squeezing his other hand. "I told you I wasn't stupid."

Thomas raised the Needle above his head as cheers erupted from Richie, Boris, Otto, and Kasha on the deck of the *Conch Whistle*.

We have a chance, he thought, smiling a broad, hopeful, uncharacteristically Thomas Creeper kind of smile.

XII

Wild Death

In the Viewing Deck of the *Conch Whistle*, Richie brought up a map of Gloomsbury on the computer screen. Boris, Thomas, and Jeni stood by his side, peering at the map over his shoulder.

"Now we just have to find the Sieve's lair," Richie said grimly. "No doubt it will be a safe and secret place, away from prying eyes, but close enough so that they could slip into town to prey upon its citizens."

An image flashed on the screen of an aerial view of a large facility with a smokestack billowing dark smog. "The Sneed factory is one possibility," Richie mused. "Perhaps the Sieve have dug a series of secret rooms under the factory floor."

"I don't think so," said Jeni. "The Sneeds are more paranoid about security than the Sieve. No one's seen old man Sneed in thirty years, but he keeps a close watch on everything he owns and everyone who works for him. All the Processing Scholars who get chosen for internships say that there are hundreds of cameras everywhere. Not really the best place for a secret cult of killers with glowing arms."

"Point taken," said Richie frowning.

Thomas wracked his brain. He knew nearly every inch of Gloomsbury. Crowley had appeared to him in the cemetery, he recalled. Perhaps their base was located under one of the mausoleums. The ground was soft, great for digging holes. Headstones collapsed on a daily basis. And when the Sieve snatched Jeni from Parishioner's Walk, it had appeared that they'd moved through the network of sinkholes.

"When the Sieve took me on their boat," said Jeni, finger

propped under her chin, "I remember the hull of their boat was covered in some kind of white mud. It got all over my shorts as they pulled me over the side."

"Brilliant!" Richie exclaimed. "We can run all kinds of tests on the mud, figure out where the boat is being hidden...Perhaps their base is located in the same place. Where are your shorts, my dear?"

"Otto told me he was going to wash them with the rest of my clothes..." said Jeni, biting her lip.

"I left Otto just a moment ago; he was heading off to do the wash," said Richie. "He was going to try to get the algae spores out of Boris's hammerhead helmet."

"Don't worry!" cried Jeni. "We're on it!"

"There's a chute off the mess hall!" said Richie. "It's the fastest way to get to the laundry room. If you hurry, you might be able to stop the wash in time!"

Jeni and Thomas took off, racing through the submersible's byzantine corridors, until they arrived, chests heaving, at the mess hall.

"Where's the chute?" Thomas wheezed, trying to catch his breath.

"Over there!" said Jeni. "In that alcove by the galley!" In the alcove full of sacks of yet-to-be-washed laundry, they found a wide metal pipe rising up out of the floor. A ring of copper light circled the top of the pipe, but everything below fell away to darkness. Before Thomas could say, "Hot pickles!" Jeni tucked her elbows in and leapt down into the chute, letting out a shriek as she slid, which faded as she sped out of sight.

"Just give me one normal day. One day," muttered Thomas, climbing over the side of the pipe. He let go and found himself zooming down through the darkness, hands covering his eyes, screaming bloody murder. A white circle of light appeared at the end of the tunnel as Thomas flew out of the pipe...only to be caught in mid-air by a giant mechanical hand!

The mechanical hand that held Thomas by the back of his wet suit was attached to a giant spinner in the ceiling. Beneath his dangling feet, Thomas could see two tubs the size of small swimming pools, each filled with sorted laundry—whites in one, colors in the other.

"Thomas!" Jeni cried out. He glanced up, just in time to see that Jeni had been caught in another mechanical hand, before they were both tossed up into the air. Screaming, they both splashed down into a warm vat of soapy bubbles.

Thomas came up for air, wiping stinging soap solution out of his eyes. Turning around, he found Jeni spluttering behind him, a beard of bubbles decorating her chin, and her strawberry-blonde hair covered in suds.

"This…is not…" she spat. "My…idea…of a bath!"

"OH, NO, NO! *KINDER*!" Otto shouted. "STAY WHERE YOU ARE! I'LL HAVE YOU OUT AND DOUBLE-RINSED IN NO TIME!"

Before Thomas or Jeni could say "Mr. Clean" the mechanical hands (this time re-directed by Otto the Second) lifted them up and set them under two copper cylinders, where warm water gushed out from two hidden hoses. Once Thomas and Jeni has been rinsed of soap suds, the copper cylinders began to lower over them.

"Um, Thomas?" Jeni called out, but a blast of warm air cut her words short. Soon Thomas and Jeni were standing, bone dry, inside the cylinders. A light clicked on.

"I'M SENDING IN YOUR CLEAN, WASHED CLOTHES!" cried Otto.

"Clean?! NO!" cried Jeni. But it was too late. The clean, neatly folded clothes scooted in on small mobile disks beneath the cylinders. Thomas and Jeni dressed.

"Push the green button when you're dressed!" Otto yelled.

Thomas pressed the green button and the cylinder rushed up to the ceiling. Jeni stood next to him wearing her clean, dry shorts, a miserable look on her face. Otto, seated atop his mobile stool, grinned at them both.

"We came here, Otto," said Jeni, "because we wanted to stop the wash before my shorts were cleaned. They had mud on them, white mud from when the Sieve took me. We thought we might be able to trace the source of it."

"White mud, you say?" said Otto. "Probably the same mud that coats the specimen." "What specimen?" Thomas and Jeni asked together.

"*Ja!*" said Otto. "I was just coming up to share my findings with everyone, but forgot to turn the Sorter off. My apologies! You don't need to worry about those shorts, *mein Freund.* The live worm I found in Thomas's backpack will serve the purpose quite nicely."

❧

On the Viewing Deck, Thomas and Jeni watched as Otto's tool-chest hand collapsed to form a long metal pointer. On the captain's computer screen, they could see a video of the worm Otto had recovered from Thomas's backpack, the small writhing creature glowing with a faint yellow phosphorescence; an image alongside depicted the internal anatomy of the worm; a third tab on his computer screen displayed various chemical elements and two DNA helixes.

"As you can see," said Otto, waving his pointer, "the contents of the worm's stomach point to its habitat. The white mud Jeni got on her shorts contains traces of calcite and argonite. In other words: limestone."

"*Argonite,*" said Richie thoughtfully. "Thomas, what did Crowley tell you about the strange cargo on the ship?"

"He said things nested in the white powder, I think," said Thomas.

"*Nested* in the limestone," said Richie excitedly. "Of course! Why did I not think of that! It explains the sinkholes!"

"*Jawohl, mein Herr!*" said Otto. "That was my conclusion as well. But there is something else I want to show you." Otto hit a button on his mobile scooter and a new window opened on the computer screen. "Here is a specimen of your run-of-the-mill glow worm, *Lumbricus terrestris.* Here is its mapped genome." With another click, the images of the two DNA helixes appeared right next to the screen with the diagram of *Lumbricus terrestris.* "I took the liberty of trying to map the genome of our little friend here recovered from Thomas's backpack."

"And?" said Richie. "What did you find?"

"An absolute mystery!" exclaimed Otto. "The Sieve worm has a broken genome, composed of proteins I have never seen before. All of which suggests that our specimen is of alien origin."

"So, hold up," Jeni interjected. "Are you saying that the worms Crowley and the Sieve have squirming in their bodies are from another planet?"

"So it would seem," said Otto. "But I have a theory."

"Go on," urged Richie.

"By analyzing the specimen's digestive tract," said Otto, "I have discovered that the worm feeds on limestone, which allows the worm to multiply. I tested this theory on the worm from Thomas's backpack, placing it in the jar of limestone. The worm split into two worms, which then after some time became four. I separated them into groups of two, removing the limestone from one jar and leaving it in the other. The worms without limestone dissolved, as you see here."

Otto reached down into a compartment on his scooter and removed a small jar. At the bottom of the white jar a pile of white powder glowed with a faint luminescence.

"But there's nothing in there, just powder," said Thomas.

"So it needs a host," said Jeni, her finger propped against her chin. "So it's a kind of parasite feeding off the limestone *and* the host. Do I have that right?"

"No, it's *symbiosis,*" said Richie. "The worms feed off the limestone, allowing them to multiply, but at some point they need a host to preserve them when they are most vulnerable—when the limestone runs out."

"*Ja, ja!*" Otto said, nodding excitedly, his white whiskers bobbing up and down.

"In return," said Richie, turning to Thomas and Jeni, "the worms prolong the host's life. As long as the worms live, the host lives."

"So how do we defeat them?" said Thomas. "If Crowley is connected to all the Sieve and he's like the host and leader, then how do we get him when *he's* most vulnerable?" He shook his head. His brain hurt. *Hosts, parasites, symbiosis*… even for his agile brain it all seemed too much to process.

"Good question, Thomas," said Otto. "I will need some more time to solve that riddle."

"I'm afraid time is something we don't have," said Richie. "I believe the Sieve are weakened from their collective teleportation earlier today. We must find them as soon as we can!"

"Wait!" said Jeni. "If the powder in the jar isn't alive anymore, if it's just dissolved worm parts or whatever, could Mouth swallow it and tell us where it came from?"

Richie looked at Otto. "Do you think it's safe, Otto?"

"I can't say conclusively," the old engineer said thoughtfully, twirling one end of his moustache. "There could be some slight side effects. It would have to be Mouth's decision."

Hearing his name, the creature known as Mouth appeared out of a shadowed corner of the Viewing Deck. Richie leaned down as Mouth whispered in his ear.

"He says he'll do it," says Richie, "but that he'd prefer to drink something for a change. A cocktail."

"Yum," said Jeni. "A powdery worm cocktail."

❧

After Thomas and Jeni had retrieved the requested elements from the mess hall—milk, nutmeg, vanilla, and a scoop of chocolate mint ice cream—they returned to the Viewing Deck where they found Otto readying the blender. They tossed in all Mouth's requested ingredients and tipped in the jar of powdered worm bits.

The strange concoction glowed with a slightly brighter yellow luminescence (not unlike the French liqueur Pernod, which thankfully is not made out of blended worm parts).

Otto handed the concoction to Mouth, who put the brimming pitcher to his wide green lips, and without so much as a "Bottoms up!" sloshed the glowing liquid down his massive gullet. Otto took the empty pitcher while Mouth blinked his lidless globular eyes, once, twice, three times. Glowing liquid dribbled from the sides of his mouth. Mouth made a circular movement with his long tongue and the last of the ice cream worm cocktail was gone.

Waddling over to the captain's chair, Mouth stood on tiptoes and whispered in Richie's ear.

"Quarry Road?" Richie confirmed as Mouth let out a few belches that popped with phosphorescent light. Richie brought up the map of Gloomsbury Township once more on the screen.

"Quarry road...Quarry Road," Richie repeated, his dart ing eyes scanning the screen. "I don't see it anywhere."

"Wait a minute!" Jeni exclaimed excitedly. "Weiland Avenue used to be called Quarry Road because it led to a quarry outside of town. But the quarry was condemned...I saw it in a newspaper while organizing microfilm for Ms. Katz. The quarry's technically located in Marvale now, but when a ton of sinkholes were discovered, the town converted the property into a wildlife refuge so the government would have to take care of it."

"Hmm, wildlife you say?" said Richie. "More like *wild death* now, I'd say. Let me see if I can pull up a map of Marvale." He made a few taps on the captain's chair. "Here we go! Looks like it's an aerial map. Wait!" Richie paused. "How does anyone get into the refuge? It's surrounded by cliffs, created by sinkholes, no doubt. Looks like this is the only way in." Richie pointed to a long brown causeway surrounded on both sides by dense marshland.

"That's Sarah's Lament," said Thomas. "You can't go

through there at low tide. The mud is too thick. It…well… swallows people."

"Perhaps we can use a life raft," said Richie. "Otto—"

"*Jawohl, mein Herr!*" the old engineer called, his pneumatic mechanical arm raised in salute.

"What is the state of the tides now?" said Richie.

"No good! No good!" replied Otto, peering at a tide chart he had removed from his mobile stool. "The tide is going out, and we cannot go any further in without rupturing the hull. But I may have a solution!"

Otto swiveled away and sped down the hallway toward his Den of Oddities. A few clangs and crashes sounded, followed by several curses in German, but then he returned a moment later carrying a number of brass stilts.

"Like egrets and cranes," Otto said smiling, "you shall become birds of the marsh!"

Mouth took one look and slunk back into the shadows.

"It's all right, *mein freund Mouth*," said Otto. "You will keep me company. Too many nasty things for you to eat in there anyway. It would probably give even you a bellyache."

Everyone took a set of stilts from the old engineer. Otto made each of them solemnly swear on the fossilized onion loaf made by his great aunt Hilda that they would return the stilts in good shape.

Thomas and Jeni duly swore "The Oath of the Loaf," and when it was all done Richie led everyone to the main hatch. Thomas gathered the gifts from the Lady: the ring and the Narwhal Needle. Richie had fashioned a leather sheath for the Narwhal Needle, and Thomas felt very proud—and a bit terrified, too—attaching it to his belt. Thomas slipped the ring onto Jeni's finger.

"You should have this," he said.

"Thomas—"

"I have the Needle," he said. "Plus, if for some reason we get separated, you can use the ring to protect yourself until I can find you."

Jeni looked at the ring. The gemstone pulsated with a faint blue glow, as if echoing the beat of her pulse.

"It feels…like…like it's connected to me," said Jeni dreamily. "I can feel it humming…like an electrical current inside my body."

Thomas frowned. "I hope that's good."

"Me too," said Jeni. "All right, we better go."

Thomas climbed the long ladder and stepped through the hatch onto the deck of the *Conch Whistle*. Night had descended, and all about was a thoroughly murky gloom. Not wishing to arouse suspicion, Otto had switched off the main deck lights, and the flashlight on Boris's hammerhead helmet lit the path for Mulvaney's Raiders. Up ahead, past a series of jetties, they could see a cluster of cormorants, and beyond them, a narrow path of crushed white shells that led through clouds of soupy mist into the dark mouth of a cave.

"Well, my friends," said Richie. "The hour of courage is now upon us. I don't know what lies inside that place, but you can bet it's something horrible. Let's remember why we are here: to make sure no one else suffers at the hands of Crowley and his devils ever again. For Pop!"

"For Pop!" Kasha and Boris cried, raising their fists.

"For Pop!" Jeni and Thomas echoed, shaking their fists in the gathering mist.

"All right," said Richie. "Let's see if Otto worked out the kinks in these stilts. I still have a few burns from the volcanic pits in Iceland last time we used them…"

Each of the Raiders clambered on the stilts and managed their first awkward steps.

"Thomas," Otto grasped his arm just as Thomas was about to try out his own stilts. "I fixed your family heirloom," he said, handing Thomas a small metal box.

Inside, Thomas found his Aldous pocket watch gleaming as if it were new, the hands moving smoothly around the interior face. There was not a single drop of water to be seen.

"I hope you will forgive me for making a slight adjustment," continued the old engineer. "Another theory, you see. If the worms are repelled by sunlight, preferring the darkness of caves, then perhaps they would also be repelled by a solar-charged chemical? With this in mind, I made a solution from the photovoltaic cells I installed on the *Conch*'s decks from our trip around the Horn of Africa last month. Your little stopwatch is rigged now."

"You made a bomb?" said Thomas.

"*Ja! Ja!*" said Otto excitedly. "You have ten seconds. The outcome is not guaranteed, but we must try everything we can at this moment."

"Thank you, Otto," said Thomas, tucking the pocket watch into his belt pouch.

Thomas climbed down the side of the submersible and inserted his feet into the footholds on the stilts. Soon he was shakily making his way through the mud. Twice he started to go down like freshly felled timber, but ever-watchful Boris was there to catch him each time. The only one who seemed right at home walking in this precarious manner was Kasha. Born into the circus, her first steps had been on stilts. While everyone gritted their teeth and knocked into one another, she laughed and strode easily ahead through the mud, reaching the beach with time to sharpen one of her throwing knives while the others staggered in.

Leaving the stilts on the beach, they gathered at the beginning of the shell path. Thomas removed the Narwhal Needle from his pouch. Just as before, the handle reacted to his touch—shaping and reshaping around his fingers, as if the Needle were alive. Jeni's ring flashed a little brighter as she slipped her hand into Thomas's. Boris retrieved a waterproof flare from his belt and handed it to Richie. The strange mist coming from the mouth of the tunnel swirled around their feet. With hearts beating hard in their throats, they moved toward the mouth of the tunnel.

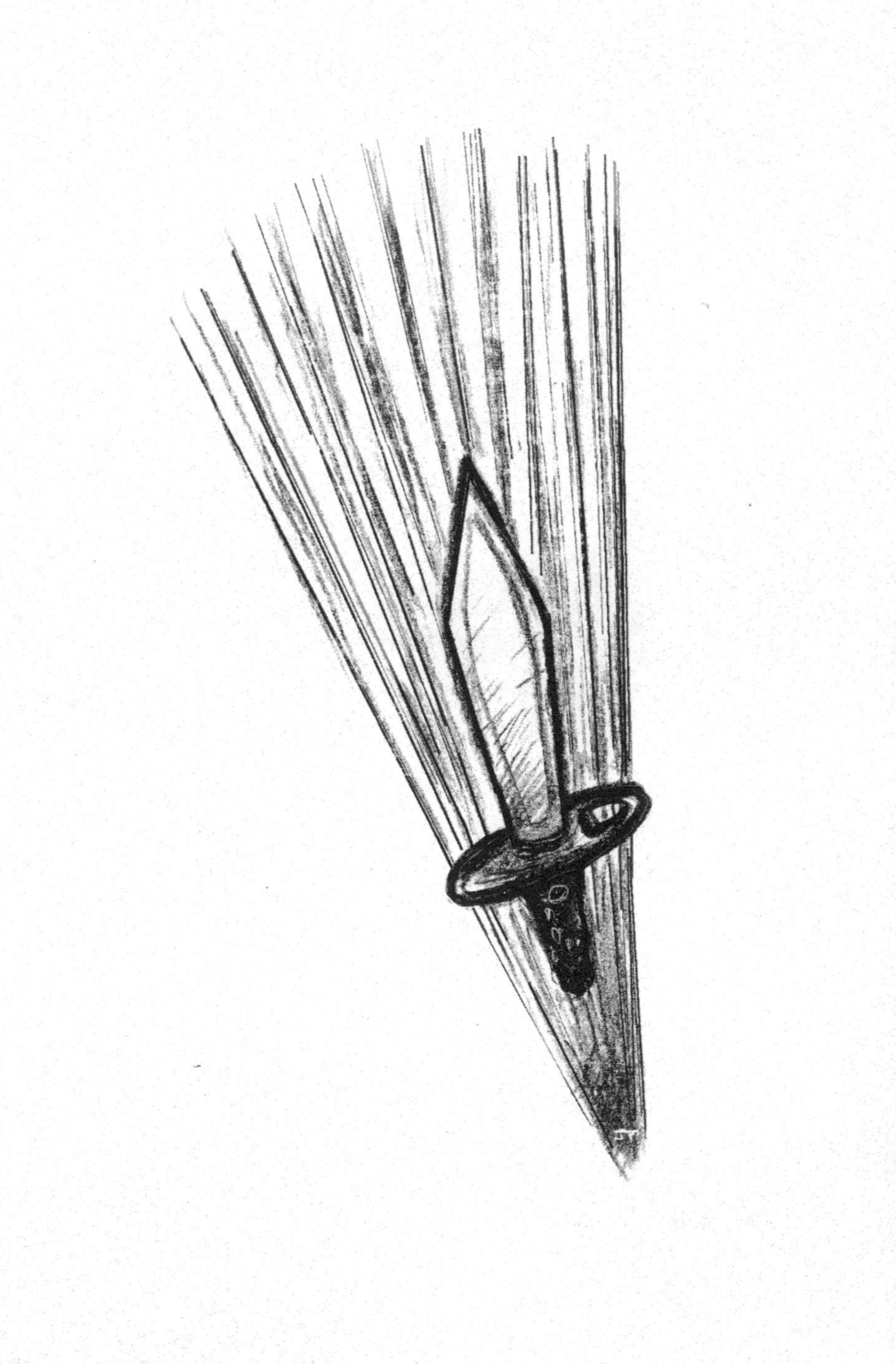

XIII

Worms

I don't think we're going to need that light," said Richie.

"*Da*," said Boris, clicking off his massive headlamp.

Thomas followed the gaze of the two men up toward the ceiling of the cave. Thousands of worms wriggled up and down the tunnel's ceiling and walls, the light from their bodies filling the room with an eerie neon glow. Thomas felt suddenly sick, as if they were within the belly of some dead animal teeming with fluorescent maggots.

"Are you all right, Thomas?" asked Richie.

Thomas swallowed hard and nodded. Jeni gripped his hand harder.

They pressed further into the glowing quarry. Seawater had spilled in from a crevice in the cliffs, filling their shoes with cold salt water. In the small pools at their feet, fallen worms squirmed like electrified leeches. Ahead, Thomas could see the original structure of a man-made room: reinforced beams, black with mold, ran in parallel strips across the ceiling. Between each dark beam, the ceiling teemed with writhing rectangles of glowing yellow worms. At the far end of the chamber a doorway opened, like the back of a throat briefly illuminated by light.

"That's the way down, I suspect," said Richie, pointing. As they approached the opening, as if sensing the departure of necessary hosts, the writhing, glowing worms began to drop, splashing down into the water.

"The worms," Boris said. "They follow us, no?"

Boris was right. Behind them the worms began dropping in greater numbers from the ceiling. They formed into twisting masses, thick as glowing pythons, and began to snake toward Mulvaney's Raiders through the ankle-deep water.

"Get off!" Jeni shrieked, kicking at a worm that had crawled up the back of her boot. Her sapphire ring flashed and the worms retreated slightly.

"They don't like the ring's light," said Richie. "Jeni, why don't you cover us?"

"Got it," said Jeni, holding the ring out before her. Like vampires feeling the sting of sunlight, the worms writhed away, swarming just beyond the circumference of the sapphire light of Jeni's magic ring. But there were too many of them. Jeni kept jerking the light of the ring around like a flashlight, but in the spaces where the light didn't touch, the worms bulged like an army preparing for attack,

"There's something up ahead," said Richie. "Stay close. Follow me!" With Jeni shielding them from behind, they took off into a run, following Richie's sloshes through the water ahead. "I think there's another chamber beneath us," said Richie. "I can see—"

But before Richie could complete his thought, they all lurched forward, the ground turning suddenly soft and spongy beneath their feet.

"No! No!" Jeni yelled. "We have to go back! The floor! It isn't limestone!"

And as if on cue, the worms beneath their feet seemed to part, as if making way for Mulvaney's Raiders who had invaded their nest. Thomas, Jeni, Richie, Kasha, and Boris all floundered frantically, falling through the disintegrating floor of worms, as if through a bowl of cold noodles. The worms slithered through their hair, into the curve of their ears, between their fingers, and beneath their clothes as they tumbled fifty feet into dark and freezing salt water.

Underwater, Thomas kicked frantically back to the surface, trying his best not to lose his grip on the Narwhal Needle. A bright blue light flashed near him and the wall of writhing white bodies around him drew away.

"Got you!" shouted Jeni, who appeared beside him, her hair wet and sleek as a seal's. Treading water, she held the sapphire ring out in front of her.

"Cover your mouth and nose!" shouted Richie. "They're trying to get inside you! I don't think they like the salt water."

Thomas looked up. From high up in the cavernous sinkhole, the worms were forming their python chains, swooping like arms to try to grasp them in the water below.

Jeni brandished her ring as one of the writhing arms scooped down over their heads. "The Needle, Thomas! Use the Needle!"

Thomas reached up, the Narwhal Needle clenched in his fist, while Jeni waved the ring around, clearing Kasha, Boris, and Richie of all the writhing worms that had surrounded them. Thomas almost cried out for joy. Not only did the Narwhal Needle cut through the worms like scissors through paper, but, just like the sapphire ring, it could repel them, sending them flying back into the walls of the giant sinkhole. But his satisfaction was short-lived. Thomas watched with a sinking heart as the worms reformed, forming an even larger arm of worms like a swirling wave. Quicker than he could yell "Hot pickles!" the worms reached out and jerked the Narwhal Needle from his grasp. The worm arm rose high up toward a ledge, the Narwhal Needle tight in its glowing grasp. A second later a glowing skeletal hand, high above, plucked the Needle from the worms.

"That is quite enough!"

Thomas stared up in terror at the familiar face peering over the ledge.

Crowley.

The ledge, also fashioned from a network of worms, lowered down and down until Crowley was positioned just above the heads of Mulvaney's Raiders as they treaded water. A wave of worms swirled around Crowley like a double helix....

A double helix! He and the worms were one, Thomas

recalled. Other figures, glowing with the same wild light, encircled Crowley, each seated on slabs of pale limestone. Crowley waved his hand and the worms flew upward, closing the hole through which Thomas and his friends had fallen, stitching up everything with their glowing white bodies, sealing them in.

"It wasn't so hard to find us, was it?" Crowley said, descending still further by a moving staircase of worms that lowered into the sinkhole. "I wonder why it took your fool of an uncle so long?"

"What do you want, Crowley?" cried Richie.

The water was freezing, and Thomas could feel a numbness seep up his spine, his legs increasingly exhausted from the effort of keeping his head above water. He felt helpless, as if he were a fish in a tank, just waiting to be plucked for dinner.

"What do I *want*?" sneered Jacob Crowley as he approached the water's edge. Worms writhed through his arms, torso, and legs, pulsing with their wild neon light. He held the Narwhal Needle in one claw-like hand. "Why, you've brought me exactly what I want! How very kind of you. Now for that other bit of trickery."

Crowley gestured with his shrunken hand toward Jeni and a wave of worms descended and wrapped around Jeni, tearing her from Thomas's side. Screaming, Jeni was jerked up into the air.

"Jeni!" Thomas screamed. But his screams were useless. With a flourish of Crowley's hand, the worm wave froze in place. Jeni tried to fight the horde with her ring. A few worms tumbled into the water, but a dozen swarmed to take their place. Without the light of the ring protecting Thomas and the rest of Mulvaney's Raiders, a thick stream of worms slipped from crevices in the sinkhole into the water, swarming around Richie, Boris, Kasha, and Thomas until they too were immobilized.

"I will have that ring now, Ms. Myers," Crowley demanded.

"Suck it, you zombie freak!" Jeni cried, swinging out with her arm and breaking away from the worm-lock to slug Crowley across the mouth. Her eyes widened in horror as his jaw broke away from his skull, leaving behind a burnt ring of dead worms. With a horrible sucking sound, Crowley forced his jaw back in place, new worms sealing over the dead ones.

"I hope you enjoyed that," hissed Crowley, "because it's the last bit of fun you shall have in your measly life. GIVE ME THE RING!" Raising a rotting hand, Crowley reached out, a stream of worms bursting from his fingers and flying toward Jeni's torso. The worms formed a rope, wrapping around her waist and pulling her closer to Crowley. Crowley grinned a horrible grin and closed his fingers over the ring, the sapphire light burning his rotted flesh all the way down to the bone. His power unfaltering, shrieking through the pain, he managed to pull the ring from Jeni's finger.

"AT LAST!" he shouted, his voice bellowing through the hollow chamber. "REJOICE, MY BROTHERS! WE SHALL SEE THE GLORIOUS PRESENT RISE! BEHOLD! WE ARE THE MASTERS OF TIME! Now, let me show you something before I kill all of you," said Crowley. "Sneed and Creeper failed you, just as Thomas Creeper will fail you again today."

At a gesture from Crowley, a curtain of worms was pulled aside as if by an invisible finger, revealing a chamber carved out of limestone. Two skeletons sat propped up against the wall, their yellowing bones still covered in shreds of clothes.

"I'd like you to meet Elijah Creeper and James Hieronymus Sneed," said Crowley. "We gave them a chance to join our cause. *Ungodly*, I believe was the word Sneed used." The Sieve brethren had gathered at the edge of their ledge, snickering and whispering in their silk-like language. "I didn't let the worms open their eyes!" cried Crowley. "They didn't deserve such glorious transformation! We choked the breath from their lungs so they could feel their god abandoning them, turning his face away from them with every breath. I think you deserve the same fate. Thomas, let's start with you," said Crowley, his eyes glittering as he directed the swirling mesh of worms like a conductor, ripping Thomas up out of the water by the neck. "I want you to feel it! Before any of them. I want you to suffer the most!"

But while Crowley had been describing the skeletal remains, Thomas had drawn out the pocket watch from the pouch at his belt. Just before Crowley pulled back the curtain of worms with his dark magic, Thomas had clicked on the stopwatch. Now, as Crowley gnashed his teeth, making a crushing movement with his hands as the worms tightened like a noose around Thomas's throat, Thomas counted in his head: *5, 6, 7*...In the light of Crowley's glowing arms he saw it: the hole in Crowley's chest and a small black shape beating behind the mesh of worms. *A black shrunken heart still beating*...

Before he reached *10* Thomas launched the pocket watch at Crowley. The watch exploded in a shower of bright particles and Crowley's wicked grin widened. The whispering laughter of the Sieve filled the cavern.

But louder than their laughter was the cry from the water below.

"ULYBNIS DRUZHOK!"[1]

A jewel-handled dagger sliced through the air, skimming Thomas's cheek, bisecting an unlucky worm, and slicing Crowley's hand from his wrist—the very hand that clutched the Narwhal Needle. Screaming, Crowley fell backwards. The worm noose around Thomas's neck dissolved into wet noodles. Reaching up as he fell, he could see Crowley's rotting hand, still clutching the Needle, fly through the air as if in slow motion. He grabbed the Needle, the handle sculpting around his fingers before he landed on the ledge a little distance from the shrieking form of Crowley. Jeni slipped from the tight web of worms and fell screaming into the water with a splash. Thomas forced himself up to his feet. *There was only one shot, one way to end it....*

[1] Russian. "Smile at this!"

Crowley held out his severed arm, worms writhing like feelers from the severed end. Thomas could see the light of the worms rebuilding themselves. Crowley whipped back his hand, readying a final storm of worm-death. Thomas raised the Narwhal Needle, then lunged forward, burying the tip deep in the hole in Crowley's chest.

Crowley's glittering eyes went white and the writhing worms under his skin stilled, their light fading to gray and then to nothing at all. Thomas removed the Needle. From the ceiling a shower of gray worms fell like rain as the light started to go out in the room. The Sieve brethren, gathered around the edges of the platform, grayed and dissolved while the platform of worms under them began to collapse. And Crowley himself was nothing more than a dissolved outline of black clothing folding inside a bed of gray worms. Thomas staggered backwards. Then the whole platform collapsed as Thomas fell into the water, sinking beneath a sea of dead gray worms.

Strong arms yanked him up as massive chunks of lime stone began to fall into the water with cannonball splashes.

"We need to get out of here, Thomas!" Richie cried. "The ceiling's collapsing!"

"I have impossible idea!" shouted Boris. "Maybe possible! Chain fingers together! Hold your breath!"

"Do as he says!" shouted Richie.

Everyone joined hands, and while stones showered down all around them, Boris dove beneath the surface. A loud slam from the far side of the sinkhole reverberated through the water, and a crack formed in the side of the chamber. With a groaning shudder, the massive rocks shifted, sending a waterfall of small stones, rocks, and dirt cascading into the water.

"What the hell is he doing?" shouted Jeni. "Is he trying to speed up killing us all?"

"No," said Richie, bobbing beside them. "I believe he's making us a new way out."

Just as Richie finished speaking, the cold water began to swiftly turn beneath their feet, as if a plug had been pulled and the chamber were a giant bathtub. Thomas could feel his body being pulled down into the sucking velocity of a whirlpool.

"Everybody hold your—"

The secret drain ripped Richie away like a ragdoll. Thomas closed his eyes as he went under, gripping the Narwhal Needle with one hand and Jeni's hand with the other. The water surged faster and faster. Something hard banged against Thomas's shoulder and he lost Jeni. They rocketed for another few seconds until a gush of water shot them out onto a sticky surface that felt like pancake batter. Thomas opened his eyes. He was lying on his back in a foot of noxious brown mud. A cormorant stood over him, a crab quivering in its mouth. They were outside.

Streaked with mud, they pulled themselves up onto their feet. Jeni threw her arms around Thomas. Boris tipped back his hammerhead helmet and rubbed his head. Richie embraced Kasha, who kissed him on both cheeks. A horn sounded out in the water.

"The *Conch Whistle*!" cried Jeni.

The tide had come in far enough so that they could see the gleam of the copper hull reflecting the first faint rays of Gloomsbury's pale sun filtering in through Mad Marge's cloudbank. Jeni grabbed Thomas's hand and together they pushed their way through the gurgling mud up onto a bank of high sea grass. From this vantage point they could see a white whiskered face rising above the main hatch, peering through one of the lenses of his goggles.

Thomas grinned. The mighty Mulvaney's Raiders looked like a cross between a rugby team playing a very muddy match and something out of a campy science-fiction film about mud people. Victory was sweet, but no one ever said anything about its having to be clean, too.

XIV

A Friend Team

The *Conch Whistle* circled back toward Gloomsbury Bay. Thomas wiped the mud off his Ken Darby Spy Watch and checked the time. It was almost five-thirty in the morning! Their parents would certainly be out of their minds with worry. They were probably combing the town, the Gloomsbury police in tow. Thomas cringed, thinking of his father's next tirade, and knew that whatever the coming punishment was, it was going to be swift and severe.

"Stop worrying so much, professor," said Jeni. "We got Crowley. You said it yourself! He was the host of the whole wormy freak show."

"Yeah, but Richie said—" Thomas began.

"I'd say Jeni is right," said Richie, appearing behind Thomas. He laughed, brushing dried mud from Thomas's hair. "Stop worrying so much, professor! The Sieve are not coming back anytime soon."

"You're right," said Thomas, looking out at the rolling surface of the ocean. He remembered the black wisps of Crowley's clothing surrounded by all the dying worms. *Who could recover from that?*

Otto and Mouth returned to the beach to retrieve the stilts. Mouth, however, became distracted by something far more appetizing: half a boat oar, which he quickly consumed. He later told Richie it had once belonged to a seventeenth-century pirate named Huck the Unlucky. Otto and Mouth also recovered two skeletons, which had been flushed out of the hole in the quarry—Hieronymus Sneed and Elijah Creeper the First! Otto made Thomas and Jeni swear "The Oath of the Loaf" that they would make sure the skeletons received a proper burial in Gloomsbury Cemetery. After all, it was because of them that Thomas and Jeni, with the help of Mulvaney's Raiders, were able to vanquish Crowley and the Sieve's murderous campaign of over a hundred years. After repeating the oath, filled with strange words in German that neither Thomas nor Jeni understood, it was time for the real gifts.

❧

While Boris and Kasha loaded the skeletons into two large nets, Richie turned to Thomas and Jeni. "The tide is coming back in, my friends, and Mulvaney's Raiders must be going out. But we can drop you within easy wading distance of the closest sand bar. I have one last surprise for you."

On deck, Otto saluted Thomas and Jeni. Surprised, they turned to discover that Boris, Richie, Kasha, and Mouth were also standing at attention, giving the same salute. Richie wore a great captain's jacket covered with patches of all shapes and sizes, with various symbols and words in different languages. He looked positively majestic, despite the clumps of dried mud that decorated his blond beard.

Thomas relinquished the Narwhal Needle to Otto for safekeeping. It was better that he kept it, Thomas thought. His mother might accidentally throw it out in a cleaning rampage. And should its powers be needed for some future crisis, Otto would keep it safe in his Den of Oddities.

"It's customary when welcoming new members of Mulvaney's Raiders to give them a gift," said Richie, retrieving two objects from a battered leather satchel at his feet. "Your paths diverge from ours, but that doesn't mean we won't be close. In the spirit of lifelong friendship and camaraderie, we give you, Thomas Creeper and Jenalyn Myers, these humble gifts—the famed Ocu-Occu Goggles for you, Thomas. May they reveal to you wonders about the dead so that you may continue to protect the living. And for you, Jeni, having lost that beautiful ring, we give you a fair consolation: a moonstone from the far side of the world. It is said to have belonged to a maharaja's wife, allowing her to see certain things in the face of the moon…"

Thomas and Jeni thanked Richie and his team for the gifts and swore to use them only for good…and certainly not to repel any annoying younger brothers with pyrotechnical obsessions. Richie hugged them both.

"Where will you go?" Jeni asked.

"And when will you be back?" Thomas asked.

"I think we need to see about that elusive sea snake in the Barrier Reef," said Richie, smiling. "If its blood can cure blindness, can you imagine the good it could do?"

Thomas and Jeni nodded.

"Don't worry!" said Richie, in his booming captain's voice. "We'll be back. And seeing that you are honorary members of Mulvaney's Raiders, who knows what adventures we'll embark upon together in the future?"

There was a great fascinating world outside the depressing clutches of Gloomsbury Township, Thomas thought. Maybe someday he and Jeni, with the help of the fantastic crew of the *Conch Whistle*, would get to see it.

After hugging Boris and Kasha, Thomas and Jeni climbed down the side of the *Conch Whistle*. Boris lowered down the two skeleton nets. Thomas and Jeni took hold of them, laughing. Quite the strange party favors to go home with!

Jeni and Thomas took one last look at the *Conch Whistle*. Saluting one last time, they turned and waded through the cold surf toward the sand bar.

"There'll never be another adventure like this in our lives," said Jeni as they watched the *Conch Whistle* slip under the water until it was nothing more than a few spumy bubbles.

Thomas yawned. "I wouldn't say that. Who knows the crazy stuff we're going to be able to see now with the Ocu-Occu Goggles and your moonstone."

"True, true," said Jeni.

They reached the sand bar and followed it to another shallow tide pool. Carefully, dragging the skeleton nets behind them, they waded through the tide pools known as Jellyfish Row. Fortunately, all of the jellyfish seemed to be the small light-colored ones, not the dark red "get the heck away from me" Portuguese Man-o-Wars that can ruin your whole summer.

When they finally reached the beach, Thomas could see a number of cars crowding the entrance, and scores of people milling around—a whole neighborhood task force. Thomas's heart sank. The dream was over. Reality was setting back in with all its depressing clarity.

"Wait one second," said Jeni. "I wanted to tell you something…something I've been thinking for a while."

"Jeni, stop," said Thomas. "I lied before about not cracking your cipher. And I've thought about it a lot. I like you…" He stumbled on the words. "A lot…I also don't want things to get…weird, you know. I just want to be able to come over and do the things like we used to and I don't…" He was rambling. He felt exhausted. His mind couldn't process one more bit of drama, good or bad.

"Hey, it's okay!" said Jeni, patting his arm. "We make a good team…I mean a good…*friend* team. I'm not sure about the boyfriend-girlfriend thing. Let's just see how things go. Can't be much more difficult than…say, defeating a group of worm-infested freaks?"

"Yeah," said Thomas, feeling strangely relieved.

Jeni laughed, the pure Jeni Myers giggle that Thomas loved. They walked the rest of the way through the surf, holding hands and dragging the skeletons behind them. Thomas could see Chip Korvin, the town sheriff, directing people here and there as they all combed the beach. *Oh great*, Thomas thought. *Here we go.*

"It's—" began Jeni.

"Yep," said Thomas.

Gary Korvin had spotted them.

"Over here! I see them!" he shouted.

Gary ran toward Thomas and Jeni at full tilt, the same insane expression on his face as he'd had at the Gloomsbury Pumpkin Festival when he told Thomas to "run from his fiery javelin." But when he skidded to a halt before Thomas, his face went white.

"What the hell is that, Creepy Thomas?" Gary gasped, pointing a shaking finger at the nets of bones.

"Nothing much," said Jeni, ignoring Gary's shocked looks. "Just the skeletons of two missing Gloomsbury residents. Pretty famous ones, too," she added nonchalantly.

Sheriff Korvin strode across the sand, speaking into his walkie-talkie: "Call it off! We got them—" And the sheriff stopped short, kneeling down to inspect the nets. "What the—?" he exclaimed in shock. Then, into his walkie-talkie: "Sharon, ah, can you wake up the coroner and send him down here? I'm looking at some nets…full of bones. Human bones. Sharon? Hello? Come in, Sharon?"

A wild conversation sounded on the end of the walkie-talkie.

Bones? Nets full of bones? Down by Town Beach?

As the chatter got louder, Sheriff Korvin turned to Thomas and Jeni. But before he could get a statement, Thomas's mother came bounding across the sand dunes, trailed by a disheveled Elijah Creeper the Fifth in his night robe.

"Thomas!" Mrs. Creeper shouted, gathering Thomas into her arms. "I thought…" she sobbed into his neck. "I thought I had lost you, too."

"I'm sorry, Mom," said Thomas, hugging his mother tight. "I can't explain everything now, but you have to trust me. I had to see about something. I had to make sure it was gone forever—"

"Thomas Creeper, by all the laws of Massachusetts…" Elijah Creeper the Fifth began.

But Thomas cut him off before he could go any further.

"Wait!" said Thomas. "Listen! There's someone I want you to meet."

"What?" his father spat. "This is hardly the time…"

Thomas dragged the skeleton net into the flashing lights.

"Dad, I would like you to meet Elijah Creeper the First. Or maybe this is James Sneed. I'm not sure. Anyway, we found them both, Jeni and I."

Jeni, who had watched the Creeper reunion wide-eyed, waved a wordless goodbye to Thomas. Having spotted her own parents coming down the boardwalk, Arnold trailing behind them, she took off.

Thomas's father gazed, astonished, at the bones in the net, his mouth open in mute surprise. For the first time, in all the years of Thomas's childhood, Elijah Creeper the Fifth was speechless.

More cars arrived at the beach, parking along Weiland, and Thomas could see the news crews from the latest sun sighting unload from a van, carrying their gear. He groaned, desperately wanting to sleep.

"What's with the goggles?" asked Mrs. Creeper, pointing to the great Knutson Ocular-Occult Goggles dangling from his belt.

"Nothing," said Thomas. "Just something I found washed up on shore."

Epilogue

Unfinished Business

Thomas's father spoke not a word on the drive home. But before they got out of the Customline, he smiled and awkwardly patted Thomas's hand.

The two skeletons sat in the back seat, their salty aroma filling the car. Thomas tried not to think about what his father would say when he finally built up the courage to tell him he didn't want to be a mortician. For the time being, he focused on that smile, that rare jewel of an Elijah Creeper the Fifth smile.

Thomas half-walked, half sleep-walked up the staircase into his bedroom. Not caring that he was still covered in mud, he unstrapped his belt and collapsed on the bed. He sank immediately into an exhausted, dreamless sleep, one that swallowed him up entirely like a sea of quiet dark.

After sleeping for an entire day, he awoke to hear his parents fending off interview requests from reporters. Thomas grabbed his backpack and stuffed it full of the necessary items: the Ocu-Occu Goggles, a flashlight, a bolt cutter from the shed, and the tin of Ströher's pretzels in case he got hungry. He wished he still had the penknife. But it was somewhere on the bottom of the ocean. He would have to tell Uncle Percival someday. But something told him the story might be worth losing a penknife over, and his literary uncle, he knew, would agree.

As his parents fended off reporters on the lawn, with Uncle Jed periodically lifting up his mask to scare away any persistent newshounds, Thomas wrote a quick note. He explained that he'd made a promise to a friend, one he had to keep, and that he would be back in time for dinner. Leaving the note on the foyer table, he darted out the back door.

Silvie met him in the back yard. She wasn't going to let him off the hook, even after the greatest, most harrowing adventure of his young life.

Are you ready? her soft voice whispered in his brain.

"Ready as I'll ever be," said Thomas. "We're just recovering a bone from some old tomb. How hard could it be?"

You'll see, said Silvie, flashing him a look. An uneasy feeling began to grow in the pit of Thomas's stomach. *Fingal's got a bad feeling about this. So do I.*

They walked rapidly through the darkening streets of Gloomsbury. Thomas could see the glow of ghost-dog Fingal moving through the bushes. Sets of giant paw prints appeared in the damp dirt of neighbors' yards, as if an invisible rhinoceros had broken free from the state zoo. At the door to the largest mausoleum in Gloomsbury Cemetery, Thomas began to think that maybe Silvie and her ghost-dog were right. But he had made a promise, and he owed Silvie his life.

"There's a light on inside," whispered Thomas. A soft yellow light spilled through the crack beneath the mausoleum's copper door.

I told you. The magician is powerful. Whatever he tries to get you to do, Thomas, you mustn't let him. Promise?

"Promise," said Thomas. He turned the flashlight off and put it back in his backpack. Removing the bolt cutters from his pack, Thomas cut through the old chain lock that secured the door.

"Tell me again why you can't come in?" said Thomas.

He's put hex spells all over the doorway. Only the living can enter.

"Well, isn't that great," said Thomas. He took a deep breath and opened the door. What he saw as the door creaked open froze him in his tracks.

Instead of a freezing, dark mausoleum draped in cobwebs

he found himself in the warm, welcoming room of a rustic cottage. A fire roared in the grated fireplace, and comfy chairs and a sofa had been invitingly positioned in front of the fire. A balding old man, with a plump red nose and laugh lines that curled down both cheeks, sat on the sofa. He wore a pale Seersucker suit with a bright red bowtie and brass buttons that caught the light of the fire and dazzled in Thomas's eyes. He closed the book in his lap and glanced up as Thomas stepped into the room.

"Finally!" said the man in a hearty voice. "Come in! You wouldn't believe how long I've been waiting for you, Thomas Creeper."

"How—how do you know my name?" said Thomas, gaping in astonishment.

"Who doesn't around these parts?" said the old man chuckling. "The boy who vanquished the Sieve and discovered the missing skeletons of Sneed and Creeper! You're practically a legend around this cemetery! But do come in. I won't bite. Come sit down over here."

"I'm fine right here," said Thomas.

"Suit yourself," said the man. "I'm sure your companion outside has told you all sorts of dreadful lies about me. That I would try to trick you? What nonsense! Come here!"

"How are you able to do all this?" said Thomas, still amazed at the transformation. Bright yellow curtains hung at a large picture window. Thomas did not see the mist and gloom of the cemetery outside, nor did he see the noxious mounds of scabber weed; instead, he saw a peaceful forest glen with a bubbling brook. He rubbed his eyes in disbelief. "Isn't this supposed to be an old tomb? How did you change everything?"

"Magic, my boy," said the old man. "*Not* illusion. The genuine article. Here! Catch!"

The old man tossed a small gold object across the room. Thomas caught it. It was a golden truffle.

"Open it!" said the old man. "See for yourself!"

Thomas slowly unwrapped the golden foil to find a perfectly carved chocolate truffle seashell.

"Taste it!" said the old man excitedly. "Go on! I assure you it is of the highest quality that would make the best Swiss chocolatiers throw in the towel and become bank tellers!"

Thomas raised the chocolate to his lips but some secret warning bell went off in his head. He lowered his hand and shook his head in an effort to clear his mind. He shouldn't be here. Maybe there was another way to help Silvie."Thomas, you are wasted as a mortician's apprentice. Why not become mine? Learn from me the arcane roads of magic. Go wherever you like! *Be* whoever you want to be! I know you are miserable. But I can offer you the chance to step away from it all, to lead the life you were destined to lead."

"You could do that?" whispered Thomas. "How?"

"Join me here," said the old man, "and I shall show you how to change minds, to make forces bend to your will, so that you will never be governed by them again."

Be whoever he wanted to be? Travel strange roads of magic to new places? For a second Thomas found himself pondering the old man's offer. It would be so easy just to close the door on Gloomsbury, on Creeper & Sons, and go to places where the sun always shined. Without thinking, he moved across the room toward the old man. Then he thought of the evil magnetism of the wire-rimmed spectacles, and how they had overtaken his will, his very self. *Was this not the same dark magic at work?*

"NO!' Thomas shouted. "Anybody who would harm a little girl and poison a dog could never teach me anything worth learning! I will take that bone back now, please."

The old man laughed. The light flickered wildly in the fireplace.

"Which one, Thomas Creeper? I have so many!"

The old man pointed to the fireplace. One by one the warm bricks of the fireplace and mantel disappeared. In their place Thomas saw dozens of stacked skulls and bones.

"Which one, is it, Thomas?" said the old man, smiling impishly. His teeth seemed to have grown longer and were now chipped, black, and dripping with saliva. Thomas recoiled in disgust.

"I-I don't know," stammered Thomas.

"I don't know," the old man mocked in a singsong voice. "You don't know, you fool! And now you are going to join my collection!"

The old man leapt from the sofa, lightning crackling from his fingertips. But before he could reach Thomas, a green emerald light poured from Thomas's chest. He fell backwards a few steps as the wild light left him twirling and gathering until it formed the shape of a beautiful woman in a flowing green dress.

Our Lady of the Waves.

The old man gnashed his teeth, but with a wave of the Lady's hand, the crackling lightning in his fingers turned to smoke. "Impossible!" he screeched. "You salty witch! You stole it! You stole my magic!"

The magician let out a piercing scream and slumped to the ground. As his body fell, the room began to change: the light went out in the fireplace; the bones clattered to the ground. The chairs and sofa disappeared and were replaced by a long black coffin. With a wave of her glowing hand, the Lady lifted the body of the magician and deposited it back into its coffin. She whispered a few words and small green ribbons of light closed over the hinges of the coffin, sealing it forever. The Lady then turned to Thomas with a smile. Her silken voice, blending harmoniously with the rush of breaking waves, sounded in his mind:

I placed a protection spell on you, Thomas, when I touched your cheek underwater. I knew it would serve you well one day. Now take Silvie's bone. It's right there at your feet.

Thomas looked down. A long white bone, severed at one end, lay at his feet. Thomas knelt down and took the cold bone in his fingers.

You were true to your word, Thomas, said the Lady. *You do want to help people. I see a bright future ahead for you. There will be more tricksters and challenges on the road ahead but I know you will do what is right. Now go! Return the arm to that poor girl and set her free.*

And with those words the Lady vanished.

Outside Thomas found Silvie in a patch of moonlight, her teeth gleaming white in a wide smile.

You did it, Thomas! You kept your promise!

"I guess…I did," said Thomas handing the bone over to Silvie. It leapt from his fingers, hovering a moment in the air before reattaching to the jagged end of the severed arm. Thomas watched dumbstruck as the red tendons sealed back together. As soon as the mending was over, Silvie started to fade.

I'm leaving you Fingal, Thomas! He says he wants to stay with you. Take care of him. And take care of yourself. Goodbye! And thank you!

"Goodbye," Thomas whispered as Silvie's image faded until there was nothing but the gloom of the mausoleum and the sound of the wind sweeping through the rusty fence.

Pawing the dirt at his feet was Fingal, the ghost-dog, glowing with an eerie green light.

"Fingal?" said Thomas. "That's rather formal, isn't it?" The ghost-dog cocked his head to one side.

"How about Finn?" said Thomas, smiling.

The ghost-dog grinned wetly, tongue lolling out one side of its massive mouth.

"I thought so," said Thomas. "Come on. Let's go home."

Then Thomas got an idea. He took the Ocu-Occu Goggles from his backpack and fit them over his head. A dead world bathed in eerie green swirled before him. Spirits sat, cross-legged, on the headstones and hovered in twos and threes at the rusty cemetery gate. They wore all sorts of strange clothing—elegant ghosts with long top hats and old tuxedos; ladies with bobbed haircuts and giant parasols; children peeking out from behind graves, smiling shyly at Thomas.

As he and Finn trudged through the wet grass, a ghost flew over and settled by his side, jabbering in Thomas's ear. He had been slashed down the middle, and dark guts hung loose about his waist. Thomas drew back, horrified at the sight. Finn, at his side, growled softly in his throat.

"It's all right, boy," the ghost said. "Tell your wolfhound I mean no harm. I had an accident at the mill," the ghost continued. "I need you to help me find the screws. They're under the floor. You see, the blade came loose—"

"I'm sorry," said Thomas. "I can't help you. Hey! How can you talk to me? I thought I needed your—"

"Artifact of Unlocking?" said the ghost. "Not all of us. Some of us are just dying to talk! Har! Har! Har!" The ghost paused to move his guts to a more comfortable position. "Say, you're Thomas Creeper, the new Fixer, aren't you? A Spirit Saver?"

"I don't know what you're talking about," Thomas muttered. "You must have me confused with someone else."

A ghost-woman in a red-stained nightgown swept over to the gutted ghost. "Says he isn't a Fixer," he muttered to the ghost-woman. "You believe that? Just helped that girl *unlock* and *transcend* and says he isn't a Fixer! Bah!"

Eager to leave the gathering of ghosts behind, Thomas took a different route home. He turned left down Weiland and crossed over Thayer until he arrived in the heart of The Uppercrust. He headed down the block, pausing at Jeni's house.

He pushed the Ocu-Occu Goggles up onto his forehead. There was a light on in Jeni's room. If he didn't have the most horrible aim in the world, he might have tried to throw a pebble up at the window. But with his luck he'd probably end up breaking it. He kept on walking. Finn, meanwhile, had taken a liking to the shrubbery in Jeni's front yard. With an excited bark, he leapt over the fence and started digging under the wilted bed of marigolds.

"Finn, no!" Thomas cried. "Come back here!"

"Hey, professor!" Jeni opened her window, having clearly heard the ruckus outside. "You're not going on another adventure without me, are you?"

"No…well…yes, I mean, I guess," Thomas stammered. "I had to keep a promise to Silvie."

"Girlfriend of yours?" said Jeni, cracking a smile.

"No," said Thomas. "She's a ghost. This evil magician poisoned her dog and then made it bite her arm off. It's a long story. And tell your parents sorry about the yard. Silvie's dog makes a real mess. He's a ghost, too. You'll meet him later. All right. Goodnight, Jeni. Come on, Finn!" Finn trotted obediently over to Thomas, giving him a chilly ghost-lick on his hand.

"Goodnight," said Jeni, distracted by the strange sets of prints appearing through her yard that didn't seem to be attached to a body. But Jeni Myers didn't believe in ghosts. Or did she?

Thomas walked home, feeling strangely peaceful and, if he didn't know better, almost happy. The rotting sign for Creeper & Sons swung gently in the wind, and Thomas thought about what the magician had said, about teaching him the "arcane roads of magic." *Could he really have left his parents behind and become someone else entirely?* he wondered.

No, he concluded. His life was pretty horrible and his family was broken. But that could change with time. He thought about the beach the morning before and the awkward pat his father had given him, and the love and relief that had flowed from his mother's hug.

Maybe the ghost in the cemetery was right.

Maybe he was a Fixer after all.

Preview of the Next Book in the Thomas Creeper Series

Thomas Creeper and the Purple Corpse

It's been a relatively uneventful couple of months in Gloomsbury Township for thirteen-year-old mortician apprentice Thomas Creeper. Sure, there's been the odd corpse here and there, but nothing malicious or vengeful, nothing like the undead Victorian death cult he and his best friend, Jeni Myers, helped vanquish at the beginning of summer.

That's not to say summer hasn't been without its surprises. The greatest one comes in the last week of August when Jeni drops the bombshell on Thomas that she's accepted a year-long athletic scholarship to train with an elite U-16 soccer squad in Germany.

Thomas does his best to be supportive of his friend, but devastation hits home like a penalty kick to the groin. A week later, to take his mind off missing Jeni and to satisfy his weekly history requirement for his home-schooling course, he boards a bus to the neighboring town of Hampswich, where an exhibit at the Alderfer Museum on Roman antiquities has just opened.

At the museum Thomas meets an elderly blind man who insists he is a tour guide. Thomas laughs at the notion until the old man confesses a secret: *he hasn't been blind all his life*, but possesses a photographic memory of everything he has seen, read, and experienced before a horrible accident claimed his eyesight. Photographic memory? Thomas is more than intrigued. The old man leaves Thomas with a card with a riddle on its face: a set of initials inscribed above an oyster shell surrounded by flames. Solve the riddle, the old man says, and he will teach Thomas how to see beyond the obvious—to become a first-rate detective.

Thomas forgets the card and the old man's offer until one morning, after a miserable ballroom dance class set up by his mother in an attempt to get Thomas to meet other kids his age, he walks home along Gloomsbury Beach and stumbles across a body washed ashore. There is something ghastly about the body: the skin has been dyed bright purple from head to toe. When a second body bearing the same purple dye washes ashore a week later, Thomas decides to accept the old man's offer. He solves the card riddle and finds himself standing in front of a door, one that he knows will change his life forever if he has the courage to open it and step inside…

Classroom Discussion

In *Thomas Creeper and the Gloomsbury Secret,* Thomas and Jeni persevere through frightening odds using a combination of book smarts and unwavering positive thinking. Thomas's selective photographic memory doesn't hurt either. I bet we all wish we had that power before taking a test!

As a classroom activity try to locate some of the different detective and spy methods Thomas and Jeni utilize in the book (Thomas's brilliant fingerprint detection using iodine fumes in Chapter Six, for example, or Pop Mulvaney's modified Caesar Shift cipher in Chapter Ten). You can even create a mock crime scene in your own classroom (BUT PLEASE! Do not harm the hamsters in the corner! They are already a little peeved by being picked up and jerked around all the time!).

For further reading on subjects that keep people like Thomas and Jeni up at night, check out some of these books from your local library. You never know…you may be a budding spy-in-training yourself. Decode the following cipher and get a clue about a central part of Thomas Creeper's next adventure in the next book in the series! (HINT: this type of cipher has appeared in an early chapter of *Thomas Creeper and the Gloomsbury Secret*).

uif Qipfojdjbo ezf, pg spcfe spzbmuz uif hpmefo bhft, ht uif nbsl boe xfbqpo pg ugf Qvsqmf Ljoh

SOME FURTHER READING

A Short List of Good Books About Spies and Spy craft—(*"Read on, Bookworms!" says Ms. Katz)*

Codebreaker by Stephen Pincock, Walker Books, 2006.

Enigma: The Battle for the Code by Hugh Sebag-Montefiore, Wiley, 2004.

Fundamentals of Forensic Science by Max M. Houck and Jay A. Siegel, Academic Press, 2006

Stealing Secrets, Telling Lies: How Spies and Codebreakers Helped Shape the Twentieth Century by James Gannon, Potomac Books, 2001.

The Poisoner's Handbook: *Murder and the Birth of Forensic Medicine in Jazz Age,* New York by Deborah Blum, Penguin Press, 2010.